The Legend of Coren

The Legend of Coren

By

Terry Lee Smith Jr.

———◆———

Illustrations By

Terry Lee Smith Jr.

Order this book online at www.trafford.com
or email orders@trafford.com

Most Trafford titles are also available at major online book retailers.

Printed in the United States of America.

ISBN: 978-1-4907-3190-2 (sc)
ISBN: 978-1-4907-3191-9 (e)

Trafford rev. 03/22/2014

 www.trafford.com

North America & international
toll-free: 1 888 232 4444 (USA & Canada)
fax: 812 355 4082

I would like to recognize my family for their continual support, including my Mother, Gwendolyn Smith. And to my dear Aunt Linda Smith, I would like to thank her for all of her efforts in continuing to help me grow as a writer.

The Legend of Coren

CHAPTER 1

THE DESERT NIGHT sky shimmers ablaze from the stars above that are within their pockets of space. To catch yourself staring above and breathing the fresh and cool air would be almost drunkenly intoxicating. Here and now is a time when people struggle to survive amongst beauty and death. It is a place where one's reality can seem to wonder like a nomad with their destination being sheer destruction. That is until reality comes back from the brink and into legend.

As legends have it: They never truly die. Rumors spread while tongues at locales remain sharper than any silver dagger. Even a whisper can breathe life into the driest of bones. To understand why stories, whether fictionalized or true, are told is to comprehend your world. It is to teach the fundamentals of right from wrong, spirituality, how to find where you fit between morality, and so on . . . The problem with stories of legends is that they are never really set in stone. Time is bitter sweet thus healing wounded memories and yet decaying all within its past. Like the desert floor of this legend, it just keeps rolling on top of itself.

In the far distance, eyes as cold as ice watch a large encampment settled on the outskirts of a ruined and long abandoned city. They belong to a pack of hungry desert wolves. The canines range in different sizes according to rank. Like the nomadic people they have been watching and traveling along side, they know and fear the desert and its blight. From the shadows, these survivors rely solely on each other and those they watch from a distance. Desert wolves are seen as kin to Tomak, a Demi god of the wild. Tomak was once peaceful to all, as *his* legend goes. At one point, Tomak was known to aid lost and wondering souls through the land; especially humans. But something changed and now the wilderness of this world has lost its way. The desert wolves' teeth begin to gleam against the moon's pale glow. They froth and stream saliva in anticipation of an opportunity to feed again on nomadic flesh.

On the grounds of the encampment, a young man by the name of Lawson is just finishing up feeding shanty-goats out by the camp's guard dog. He is reminded just how close he is to the fringes of the large camp. Though Lawson and his many other nomadic tribesmen have been here en route through their travels, they felt particularly safe keeping their precious goats away from the main grounds and towards the abandoned city. A lone howl in the distance brings a shutter to Lawson's spine. He begins to adjust his thicker outer wear that was handed down to him as a child by his Father. Like everyone that was raised there, Lawson does what he can to survive. Everyone has a task to do which benefits their tribe. As wanderers of the desert sands, they are skilled in following the stars and know a good portion of the lay-of-land. Rumors have always spoken that nomads can even sense direction by the Oracle who is the Goddess of the wind. The nomadic people: Forever searching for their place in this world.

They've been able to barter and even earn a small profit from what they've found throughout their ventures in places like the bleak city before them. But the desert is seemingly becoming more of an entity all on its own as even habitable places are being over-taken by its gritty embrace. This leaves nomads like Lawson to struggle more and more just to keep up with the pace of survival. Here, everything has its price such as a place to stay, food, water, and everything else.

Nomads are, unfortunately, as poor as they come. Ignorance follows suit when misunderstandings are not addressed. Being turned away from the rest of society because you're seen as backwards and having a lack of ambition or sense of greed in progress goes with the territory. Nomads of the desert, fortunately, are a free people. Despite the dangers that loom that are seen and unseen in a place also known as the *Center of the World*, it remains as unpredictable as ever.

The only thing Lawson truly owns to himself is his name. Seeing it as a strange name, Lawson never really cared for it. Like most nomadic people of this world, he wasn't given a last name. For many generations, his people have kept things simple. Along with respecting their surroundings, including the supernatural forces like the Oracle and Tomak and his kin, they try to remain at peace. But for Lawson, one could say he sees things "outside-of-the-box." He has dreams of beyond the sand dunes and more.

A wicked howl can be heard again which causes the guard dog to turn its head. The shanty-goats, small with their long hairs, appear unafraid. This gives some comfort to Lawson. Seeing that each goat has their share of feed, Lawson turns towards the large fire in the center of the encampment and leans against an old post. The fire isn't too far from his very small tent where his make-shift of a pouch-pocket like bed lies and waits for his return once again. And though the warm fire is large, bright, and appealing, Lawson just catches himself staring off into the celestial sky.

Lawson is reminiscing about his Mother, Sabita, who passed away when he was just 10 years old. It was from an unknown illness that was unfamiliar to his tribe. His Father, Andolin, left just before she died in search of a cure. He gathered all of the wealth he hadn't shared with his nomadic tribe and left alone through the sands. As his Mother lay dying, Andolin once told Lawson that the Gods are punishing him for his greed. That was before his fated venture from which he never returned. Lawson still imagines his Father out there somewhere traveling by the romance of the wind and stars. Yet Lawson's thoughts struggle with the duality of fantasy from reality. With his loving Mother gone and Father missing, Lawson was raised by a man named Wesley.

Wesley or Wes, as he is better known in his tribe, was an eccentric nomad. He was an outcast amongst outcasts, if you will. But eventually he too would disappear from within the sands. It was during a routine travel from one town to another when suddenly Wes was left unaccounted for. Once again, Lawson, though a more mature young man at the time, found that he was alone. Like very few people, Lawson knows how it is to feel alone in a crowded place. He gained a hard exterior and is known amongst the nomads as a quiet guy. As a nomad, that's just fine. But as a sole person, he can sometimes be misunderstood, misread, or even resented. This was brought about more so by the free thinking teachings of Wes. Wes did love Lawson like a son. Just as about as much as he loved the physical realm of science and what he could see rather that what everyone else believed.

The nomadic life is a harsh one as tribesmen alike believe in many Gods and their legends that follow to temper down their world. They have a belief for almost everything as praying for what they often times need come short-handed. Wes, on the other hand, didn't just take his eyes from the heavens and asked for rain. He was always looking beyond that and wondering what was really out there.

As Lawson grew within the care of Wes, Lawson was always astonished by the knowledge and wisdom of him. In Lawson's youth and thinking, he saw himself as an apprentice. Being with his guardian, Wes, was always more than entertaining than playing with the other children who often teased and treated him like a mat. Wes, to Lawson and perhaps only Lawson, was a genius. And though others thought he was a little crazy, Lawson saw what others couldn't; like Wes as himself.

It was Wes' theories that made him into such an outsider amongst the other nomads. He always believed that everything has its explanation. As a self-taught-man, Wes gathered things that were old and ancient while on scavenging runs. To him, these were treasured artifacts of the past. But the ones he treasured the most were books. By today's standards, the nomadic people saw them as worthless and a waste of time and resources to their survival. This not only contributed to Wes' keeping tightly to himself but also to his loneliness as seen through Lawson's young eyes.

A theory by Wes that Lawson loved very much was that their world wasn't all that they thought it was. As seen in many torn and tattered pictures of his books, Wes believed that the world itself was once a very different place with a wide variety of environments and places which were filled with many different types of people and creatures never seen before by anyone of their time. It seemed to be a world Lawson could better accept. Many of his books, though somewhat aged by time, Wes has been able to understand.

He found that ancient people were great inventors and theorized that their society was unlike anything anyone has ever seen before. Ancients could swim the deepest depths of the waters and ascend to the heavens themselves. One treasured book of Wes' has strange symbols and stars on its cover. It's very thick and intimidating as Wes has spent most of his time prodding and sifting through its many pages. With its intricate words shrouded to Lawson and Wes, it remains as foreign as ever. But to Wes its pictures said it all: That anything was possible.

The night only seems to stretch for Lawson. He gazes back while rubbing his face that feels a little numb from the chill. There, the abandoned city, with its tall structural buildings lay almost frozen in time. The tallest and most spectacular of buildings are the ones further in the distance against the largest of sand dunes; forming a canyon-like drop that is hundreds of feet down. None of the nomads have gone that far into the city in fear of the sand and structures toppling over them. For many others, they believe that some areas are intended for the Gods only. Superstition, as Wes would have put it. As Lawson was raised by Wes for quite some time, he believed in his mentor and thought the same as well.

Yet that too only alienated him more from the others. Lawson catches himself staring at the large encampment fire. There, Erika, a girl he grew up with who has now become a woman, sees his blazing eyes. Lawson's mind is on Wes and how far, if at all, he has come. She gives a brief smile. Erika is unsure if Lawson is watching her or the fire. Anyone within the tribe can clearly tell how much she cares for Lawson. That is except for Lawson himself. Lawson sees the beauty in Erika but has been too preoccupied within to give notice. She has been able to excuse the tragedies in his life and what she believes to be her own faults towards self-image.

As a fellow nomad, Erika's hands are more than familiar with work as age shall someday turn those very sweet palms of hers dry and brittle. Even now she bares slight smudges on her face from the chores of the day. Lawson's eyes catch Erika's doe-like expression upon him and in that instant, he looks away. Erika looks down and into the fire from her seating and rubs her arm timidly in response. The night seems to only last longer as clouds begin to roll about the moon; shadowing the sands below.

The guard dog yawns before settling himself down on all four legs. As the night remains quiet as the Lord of Death, Matah, an old woman approaches Erika. She is by far an elder amongst the tribes of nomads named Shay. She is also Erika's Grandmother. It takes a lot to be an elder, but most importantly is the very thought of a nomad attaining the age range of Shay in such harsh and unforgiving conditions is rare. Her political power is above the other elders and even the neighboring nomadic tribes must adhere to her thoughts and say. It was the tribesmen from the far reaches that are beyond the Center of the World who spread their belief that to live beyond one's expected life is to be touched by the God's themselves. In Lawson's tribe, that belief was further stapled when, in Shay's early adulthood, she began having visions. This was all before Lawson's birth by his Mother, Sabita.

These were indeed odd and sometimes frightening visions, in Lawson's view. In one instance, Shay has seen unknown people through the desert sands; sometimes playful and other times just more confusing. But the worst visions came to her as giant creatures and insects unlike those roaming the desert sands of today. To her they remain so real. Over the years, Lawson knows that it is more personal or worse on the elder, Shay, when it is a vision she keeps to herself.

As a high ranking elder with "visions from the Gods," that never helped the skeptic, Lawson, who was often shunned by Shay for his loyalties towards Wes who often brushed away her senses of mysticism. Shay and Wes had always quarreled their opinions and ideas to each other. Lawson had always admired Wes' thoughts on reason and fundamentalism. To him, Wes was the believer and Lawson was the dreamer. Lawson misses his quirks and awkwardness.

The old woman glances at Lawson and then stares directly into her Grandchild, Erika. Shay begins to speak softly which is just beyond Lawson's hearing. She says, "I don't have to be blessed to be in my age to know when you are distressed, my dear Erika. Tell me what troubles you." Erika looks upon Lawson then the fire again before answering, "It's nothing, Grandmother." The elder, Shay, smiles and begins to wipe the smudges from Erika's face gently and says, "The stars do not shine as brightly as you do no matter how hard this world tries to hide you. You are truly special. It is your heart that has been torn from my interference between you and Lawson throughout the years." "But Grandmother Shay . . ." said Erika who sensed that Shay was blaming herself. "No, Erika, it is true. Life is too short. I was selfish to keep you from getting too close to Lawson when in your youths. You are a woman now and you are able to make your own decisions." told Shay. Erika, still stunned by Shay's response, can feel her heart fluttering in thinking about Lawson. But still she wonders why.

Erika asks honestly, "Then do I have your permission for Lawson to have my hand and soul?" "Ah, the old institute of nomadic marriage." said Shay pleasingly. "The Goddess of love, Sierrah, will be pleased. I've had a vision about Lawson that I haven't told anyone about." "You had a vision about Lawson?" asked

Erika. Erika reveres Shay's visions like most respected nomads. Unlike Lawson or the lost Wes, she believes every word of the Gods. Shay continues, "My vision wasn't like anything I have seen before. I sense that it was about our world and everything in it: From past, to present, and to our future. As I have seen, Lawson is somehow tied into something more than I can comprehend. But unfortunately, as things go, he'll have to make decisions in order to find who he is. Be patient with him, Erika. The Gods' virtues will always find a way." "As always, Grandmother." acknowledged Erika.

Though Erika is slightly confused about Shay's vision, she respects her positive out-look. It's a sense of "what will be, will be" attitude from her Grandmother. Yet a vision that is prophetic from Shay is always un-nerving to any nomad. For Erika, it doesn't matter. She has her Grandmother, Shay's, blessing who happens to be the most respected of her tribe's elders. Come what may because Erika is in love.

Shay watches as Erika, who isn't keeping her eyes off of Lawson, stand up and walk around the fire. Lawson sees her approach and catches her smile. In return, Lawson gives a brief smile. Though he was alone and away from the others, his smile was as always warm and inviting to Erika. There is a real sweetness beneath Lawson that she can sense. Erika often wondered if things were different in Lawson's life from losing his Mother, Father, and guardian, Wes, could they really of had a life together. While most nomads would have already moved on with their lives and had families, it seems as though Erika and Lawson are continuing to dance around the flames in their hearts.

"Hey." said Lawson surprisingly to Erika. Erika halts just a little short of Lawson who is still leaning against the post. Lawson, who isn't much of a conversationalist, catches Erika by surprise. Her mind is blank and the only thing she can respond back to is a copy of Lawson's own word, "Hey." Her mind was filled with so much to say and with so much feeling for Lawson. Lawson, on the other hand, remembers the silly times they've had as a kids and all of the adventures they said they would go on while challenging the Gods themselves. Lawson says to the surprisingly quiet Erika, "Are you all right, biscuit? Why the long and sour face?" Erika giggles while saying, "Biscuit? You haven't called me that in ages. Don't call me that, Lawson. It's not funny . . ." Erika playfully belts Lawson's arm with her open palms. Lawson continues to laugh and asks, "Really now, how are things with your Grandmother?" Erika looks back at the camp fire to only see that Shay has already moved on. Erika quickly looks back at Lawson who points to her nose and says playfully, "She missed a spot." "She doesn't hate you, Lawson." "Yeah, I know." told Lawson. "Like everyone else, it's just my unusual name they hate."

Erika moves in closer to Lawson as the rolling clouds seem to reveal the moon's glow. She tells, "Grandmother Shay just wants everyone to be happy including us." Erika's eyes begin to almost shine beneath the moon as if they belong to the heavens themselves. The moment seems almost supernatural as what appeared to be the Goddess Sierrah's "touch" course through their bodies. To Erika and Lawson, it feels like a warm spark; undeniable and true. Love amongst the nomads is or should be simple. Erika understands this as Lawson can see only its complexities and loss. He imagines his Father, Andolin, now who has been searching for a cure for his wife that is long gone who of which never returned to what was left of his family anyway. Perhaps the sands swallowed him whole and alive after being lured by the cruelest of Gods. For Lawson, the skeptic, that would be the cruelest of ironies. But that doesn't matter now.

Lawson takes his gaze away from Erika's doe eyes. She is lost for words in feeling personally rejected. Erika takes in a deep breath and manages to say, "It's strange out there, isn't it, Lawson? I'm referring to those that Wes would have called 'ancient ruins' just beyond our camp. The secrets they hold must be tempting for you. Even for me, a God fearing woman, I wondered about their society and technologies. Wes said ancients could fly like the Gods themselves." "Shay and the others believe they know better and what is best." said Lawson. "Every nomad seems to believe we exist to just scavenge our past for its trinkets and wealth for our own survival. They mocked Wes unfairly and when he vanished, not a soul cared."

Erika kneels down and scoops just a bit of gravel and sand onto her hand. After coming back up, she shows Lawson what she has. Then, with her other hand, she grabs Lawson's hand and slowly sifts the gritty earth from her palm into his. Erika comments, "Don't you remember some of the first taught lessons to us as nomadic children? 'For wherever the sand goes, we go so that one day we shall all return to the sand once more.' We must all continue forward, Lawson, until it is our time when Matah comes to take our hand. And through these sands we must learn when it is time to let go and bury the past."

"You're good to me, Erika, unlike the others. I do remember everything . . ." told Lawson. "Then keep the good memories of your family at heart." spoke Erika. "And smile more. I mean it. It'll help you be less pessimistic to the world." It feels right for Erika to hear Lawson say she is good to him. While reading in between the lines, she swears she actually heard him say that she is good *for* him. Erika's wish is for her heart to stop dancing around Lawson and just walk with him hand and hand.

Her continual smile finally gets him to smile more brightly before he says, "Is there something else you wanted from me or wished to say because your eyes, though beautiful, are really strange under this moonlight, biscuit." This is her chance. "There's going to be a celebration for Sierrah tomorrow as someone will ask to take the hand of another." told Erika. Lawson asks, "Who's proposing?" Erika responds with a jovial tone in her voice, "You'll just have to come and see."

Erika swiftly turns and begins walking away lively from Lawson as she can barely hold in her excitement. Lawson watches as she turns towards her tent as she is met by Shay. He finds it to be a little strange in seeing Erika laughing and talking happily with all smiles to the elder. He can only wonder what sweet Erika could be talking about in such a manner. Seeing them disappear within the tent, eventually Lawson's mind settles and thinks nothing of it.

The night air is starting to feel stale as others within the camp head for their tents. Lawson plans on doing the same. With a big day of celebration of the Goddess Sierrah happening tomorrow, Lawson now has his mind on Erika. He knows she *is* good for him. But the past can sometimes be like a fearsome scorpion; inescapable from its claws and sting. It is hard to avoid and at worse poisonous to the soul.

Still smiling, Lawson scratches his head and looks down at the mound of sand that Erika poured through his hand on the desert floor. He says bluntly while shaking his head, "Biscuit."

CHAPTER 2

Lawson moves away from the old post and shanty goats and begins to head towards his tent where he hopes to get a good night of rest. The moon is once again in full view as the clouds slowly depart. Lawson gives out a small yawn before he catches a shadow moving swiftly from the corner of his eye. He stops in his tracks and looks back with just his head turned. Lawson sees that neither the guard dog nor the goats are aware that something is a little off. Turning his body towards the tall shadow, Lawson follows its trail towards its source. The shadow catches his mind as human which gives Lawson the confidence to see who it belongs to. Just a half torso and head are shadowed while watching Lawson. Lawson, who is blinded by the moon's light in trying to make out the figure, squints his eyes and uses his hand as a visor. What Lawson can further see are large boulders that which this person is peering from behind. As Lawson takes one step closer, he plainly sees the shadowy person kneel down from sight.

Lawson has had enough of this. He presumes they are just children from his tribe playing around. Lawson walks over towards the city entrance which requires a little climbing since it is covered by rubble and sand. While continuing his short climb, Lawson is beginning to wonder if finding who this person could be is worth the effort. Before he realizes it, Lawson is before the very boulder where the mystery lies in wait. "Alright. No turning back now." said Lawson. "Come out from there . . ." There wasn't any response or anyone listening to his command. Lawson looks back at his tribe's camp and realizes he is safe and not too far from the others. But realizing that a child from camp is missing from home because he or she wishes to play games in the dark is enough to arouse anger in Lawson. Lawson is aware that he has no family and would give anything to be with Wes, his Father, Andolin, or his Mother, Sabita.

Lawson takes a step behind the boulder and looks around. He doesn't realize that his feet aren't planted securely, which are just above a sandy and somewhat steep angled slope. A tall shadow darts from a corner within the ruined city grounds. Feeling his heart jump after taking notice, both of Lawson's feet cave into where he is standing; causing him to lose his balance and tumble downward. His thick outer-wear takes the brunt of sand and gravity's blow to the hard ground. But the sands are always deadly as some of which choke the inside of Lawson's throat. He coughs loudly on all fours with his head down to the ground. While positioning himself to a sitting stance, Lawson continues coughing.

All the while, a low growl just begins to pierce his hearing over his own loud coughing. Lawson's cough subsides before he starts dusting his hair of any remaining sand. He thought he may have been hearing things at first. That is until another grumble turns into a more sharp and deeply vicious growl to his ears.

Looking up, Lawson sees in horror the sight of a lone desert wolf. It's very large with wild, gleaming eyes that are staring down Lawson who finds himself frozen in fear. The wolf's fur is short, ragged and scruffy. Its dark appearance matches the night sky, except for the white of its teeth that it bears. The desert wolf takes a step closer towards Lawson. It sniffs the air around Lawson as if for a sign of confirmation of its next kill. Lawson senses an opportunity. He blinks once, which the desert wolf catches quickly before Lawson motions himself further back.

The hungry wolf gives out an un-nerving growl before leaping brazenly into the air and over Lawson. Lawson sees a moment when one can see their life flashing before their eyes in an almost slow motioned cinematic scene. Lawson thinks about his Mother, Sabita. She was a beautiful woman whose kindness also matched her grace. His last memories of her he'll never forget. When she became ill, Sabita once told Lawson to not worry because one day they shall all meet again. Lawson can practically smell Lord Matah all around. If this was it, he was more than ready.

As the desert wolf's claw-pounce comes just inches from Lawson, Lawson closes his eyes. From the dark corners of his eyelids, they are suddenly filled with a bright light. Lawson can feel a strong surge of wind rush about his torso and head followed by a deep **YELP** coming from the desert wolf. Sensing that he is still alive, Lawson opens his eyes. What he first sees before him is the wolf lying several feet from where Lawson struggles to get on his two feet. Still feeling shaken and with his heart pounding, a feminine hand reaches out to Lawson. Lawson takes the hand with little hesitation.

Lawson gazes onward at his apparent savior. As his eyes continue upward, this mysterious person wears rugged jeans held together by a black belt that Lawson barely sees which peaks from a long and thin coat. Lawson gets back on his feet to see that this person is wearing a red bandanna just below the eyes which covers the nose and mouth. "Who are you?" Lawson asked timidly. There is no answer beneath but a gust of wind which fills his savior's coat. The cool air picks up and swirls it in a funnel pattern that Lawson has seen many times. The whirl of wind and sand intensifies as it seemed to move with force from a controlled presence. Lawson steps back while the other before him stands ground. The small twister moves over and hovers about the downed body of the desert wolf. Lawson's eyes widen at the sight of what he is witnessing. The wolf's hide begins to bulge into a more human-like form; sprouting longer limbs with digits.

It's strange for Lawson to see such a sight. He's heard of the legends of man-beasts and beasts of men yet he never could imagine that his own story would now be written. The mongrel stands tall on two legs. It still bares most of the short and scruffy fur of a desert wolf. From Lawson's perspective, it remains shadowed beneath the night sky. It begins to look around while sniffing the air loudly as if it is unfamiliar to its surroundings. Taking in a better and stronger smell towards the two, its eyes set a wide gleam at them that is wild and bright. It lurched and breathed harder which showed its flexing back muscles. The man-beast's stretched mouth, just beneath the nose, begins spiting foam until finally speaking in a deep voice from within its belly and says, "Coren, from the last time I've seen you I believe you have taken something of value from me." The beast takes a step further while uttering, "I know it is you behind that mask and disguise, Coren. I can smell you from anywhere my kin are. And whatever they see I can see."

Just moments before the claw-bearing creature spoke, the surrounding city becomes alive with gleaming eyes from the shadows of the ruined city. They never seem to blink as their presence becomes better seen as they walk towards and surround Lawson and Coren. They're hungry desert wolves. Lawson feels as though he escaped one fate just to be brought on to another horrible demise. "Stay close to me, Lawson." said Coren. "You're a woman?" said Lawson ever so innocently. It hasn't occurred to him yet how Coren has come to know his name. Not ignoring such bigotry, Coren gives out an exhausted huff and takes off her red bandanna. Lawson can see that she is pretty and must be roughly about his age. She has straight head-length blonde hair that is cut at a diagonal angle at the back. Nothing too odd by today's standards since most folks have their own style. Lawson has a sense of trust about Coren. But how could she do anything against so many?

Coren says to the slow approaching beast, "Tomak, these cuffs I bare do not belong to you nor anyone. Now I say they are mine! And if you have a problem with that . . ." "The boy may have a problem with that." answered the man-beast Tomak. "I've heard you've gone through great lengths to find him. It would be ashamed if something were to happen to him." As Tomak stops in his tracks, the desert wolves begin to slowly close in. Coren, who looks about, once again continues to hold her ground. Lawson finds himself against a "wall" as he moves closer to Coren. "What's going on? That can't be the *real* Tomak. This just can't be happening." Lawson confessed out of fear. "Stay low." ordered Coren. "You're about to see what this girl can do."

The first desert wolf attacks. It lunges straight for Coren. She ducts while throwing her thin coat about the would-be killer. After quickly releasing her grasp on her coat, the wolf, who is now just behind Lawson, is struggling feverishly to find itself out of the coat. Lawson witnesses Coren unsheathe a short-sword, which is larger than a dagger yet smaller than a sword, and burry it in the wolf through her own attire. Another hound of the desert races towards Lawson, this time. With its teeth, the desert wolf pulls Lawson away from Coren by his long and thick outer wear he has had since childhood while two other wolves dart into the chaos. "Coren!" yelled Lawson helplessly. "Lose the clothes, Lawson!" ordered Coren. As Lawson fumbles with his handed-down attire, he finally realizes that Coren knows his name, questionably.

Lawson is able to get his outer attire off. His fear leaves him as if he was on fire by the desert wolf's deadly pull. Coren knows that with Tomak inhabiting the form of a desert wolf's body in present, she will have to stand her ground firmly or lose the life of Lawson. Tomak's influence on the wolves appears to make them subjugated and unlike any normal animal of the wild. At his command, Coren has witnessed wolves of every type act more brazen while attacking at Tomak's will.

Coren quickly puts down the nearest desert wolf with one blow to its skull. She then pushes Lawson aside from another leaping attacker. Lawson sees Coren, as he smacks into a large boulder, take a long swing at the wolf which then takes its life quickly. Coren's head looks towards the dark recesses of the ruined city. She says, "We won't last long here. We'll have to move. Are you up for this, Lawson?" Lawson senses a once in a life time opportunity as a gap forms amongst the creeping desert wolves. He then looks upon Coren and nods his head for the go and for what must be done. Sweat begins to form about his face. The wind catches the scene again; whirling about every one and creature that is present.

He dashes fast. Faster than what Coren expected, Lawson's feet almost seemed to daringly float above the grounds. The rocky and graveled ground couldn't and didn't stop his sail. Coren gives a wicked smile and says to herself, "That's my boy." She then follows on after Lawson with her short sword in tow.

Coren sees Lawson's brave heart that did not miss a beat. The desert wolves begin closing in the surrounding circle they created. Their paws thump and scrape the sand-taken ground while growling and breathing heavily for their meat. Coren is clearly faster than Lawson as she is able to catch up to his side. She looks on at the meek Lawson in awe as two wolves clash into each other in an effort to achieve a kill. Lawson looks on at Coren with the wind in her short honey hair and a killer's smile on her sweet face. To him, Coren appears to be enjoying herself.

In Lawson's mind, the plan is to run into the dark areas of the ruined city and find a suitable place to hide. "Lawson, get ready!" yelled Coren. They're still too short of the city's depths. What could this mysterious woman have in store for Lawson? Coren, while still on the run, begins moving her arms out in front of herself which goes un-noticed by Lawson. She moves her arms and hands in a swirling motion. From the corner of Lawson's eye, he catches the black wrist-cuffs on Coren begin to glow brightly. Tomak wildly pushes a yelping desert wolf from out of his path in anger. "You have interfered one too many times, Coren!" bellowed Tomak. "You have no right to take my cuffs!"

Just a few feet before Lawson and Coren, where the shadows of the city remain dark as the night sky, a portal materializes. "There Lawson, is our salvation." told Coren in a huff. "Take my hand and trust me!" As Lawson grabs Coren's hand, Coren uses a good amount of her strength to toss Lawson into the whirling and bright abyss. Coren then stops to take in a moment in order to look Tomak directly into his brightly gleaming eyes. She slowly walks backwards towards the portal. In the utmost of defiance, she then sticks her tongue out from the corner of her mouth in a playful manner with her head slightly tilted. She lastly steps into the other side of the oddly stretched doorway before it vanishes without any trace of the pairs' existence.

Lawson finds himself lying face down on top of grass and dirt. While picking his head up, gusts of wind crosses through the grass which gives it a wavy appearance against Lawson's face. He sees a white flower that he hasn't seen before which blows closely to where he lies. The flower's dance against the "Oracle's wind" can be seen leaning against its own shadow. Looking straight ahead, Lawson sees the sun beginning to rise which causes the pale flower's shadow to hide. Lawson feels his head with his palm while he attempts to regain standing on his two feet. A slender hand reaches out for him in a helping manner. As he finds himself once again letting his guard down to receive help from this mysterious person, Lawson ignores the fact that it led to danger. The first thing he thinks about is the grass. He can't remember when the last time he saw so much of it at once.

"Now, Lawson, I know what you must be thinking." told Coren. "This must be all too much to ingest all at once." Lawson bends down against the wind while touching the green grass that is low. Coren frowns in question of Lawson's non response. She says, "Oh, I get it. It's been a while since you've seen the grass, huh? Well then, take a look around. We're not in the Center of the World any more, Lawson." Lawson looks towards the direction where Coren is standing. Behind her are large trees that seem to stand against rocky and hilly terrain. "Where am I?" asked Lawson. Coren answers, "Somewhere that's very far north and away from the sands. Look over there, Lawson." Coren points to where the grassy ground that they are standing on ends. Lawson walks just a little ways before the cliff drops. Before him is the most beautiful sight he has ever seen. Against a rising sun remains a valley full of life. As a flock of birds whirl past his sight, it could not deter him from looking on with wide eyes.

There he sees trees that stretch out for miles as bush after bush dot and smother the scene with greenery unlike anything he has seen before. But most shocking to Lawson is the large stream of water that snakes and crosses between the trees. From as far as he can see, the crystal waters almost appear to be coming from the sun itself.

"Heaven" is the word that comes to Lawson's mind. His nomadic people have a term for where the good and righteous will end up some day after they have passed on. Lawson is currently feeling unworthy of such a sight. Especially after seeing Tomak first hand and surviving his onslaught. This is like a place he sometimes imagined he would see his Mother again. It is a place where the water flows as freely as the people who come to drink from it. Lawson then remembers a book of Wes' where the pictures showed such valleys. That particular book also seemed to highlight many fruitful trees that were cut down by the masses. This leaves Lawson with only more questions on spirituality and life as he knows it. If only Wes could witness what Lawson is seeing now.

Coren walks up beside Lawson and places her palm on his shoulder. She says, "'Beautiful, isn't it? But I didn't choose this spot simply for the scenery. Sometimes I like to call this spot my 'little get-away' from everything. Come on, I'll show you where I stay." As Coren begins to walk away from the magnificent view, Lawson asks, "Why am I here?" Coren stops in her tracks and breaths deeply before answering, "It's a long story and perhaps one that is long over-due." "Yes, a few explanations are at least owed to me. For instance who are you and was that really Tomak?" Lawson asked out of frustration. Coren looks back at Lawson who has his arms crossed. She takes in another moment to think. It may not seem like it but, to Coren, time is precious. In one moment there would be too much to tell. Even if it's about who and what she is. She knows just what to say to keep Lawson moving.

Coren says, "It took me a long time to find you, Lawson. When I was told you were a nomad, I searched every end of this world just for you since nomads never stay in one place for too long. I know of you, Lawson. It was Wesley who told me what he knew. He's in danger and I need your help. So what say you, Lawson? Are you in?"

CHAPTER 3

"WHAT DO YOU mean Wes is in danger?!" asked Lawson loudly. "For that matter, how do you know of him?" "Come, Lawson." ordered Coren. "At that much I can explain." As they begin walking, the scenery to their right, though beautiful, catches Coren and Lawson in different moods. Lawson's mind is just catching up with him. After encountering the vicious desert wolves, flying head first through a mysterious portal, and getting word that his guardian and mentor, Wes, may be in danger begins to cloud and race his thoughts.

Coren, on the other hand is more concerned with keeping Lawson alive. His piece of mind is the least of her troubles. Coren has been around for a long time. Only she and a few others that are like her can remember the days when the world was very different. Lawson stops and asks, "What is this place?" She answers, "I told you it's my little 'get-away.' You can stay as long as you like."

Before Coren and Lawson stands a dilapidated spire made of mortar and large bricks. Lawson can see a demolished stairway that was once in a spiral leading to a frameless window that over-looks the valley. "I spent many evenings staring out of that window. That is until that stair case fell from under me. 'So embarrassing. Things just aren't what they used to be any more." told Coren. Lawson interrupts and asks, "You live in this thing?" "I sort of do." smiled Coren. "Well, more like underneath it. This was all part of a larger place at one time."

She points to a round and sealed entrance-way on the ground. "You want me to go down in there?" Lawson asked in doubt. "With you?" "Will it make you feel any better if I took out my short-sword and went first?" Coren asked. Lawson takes in a moment to think. Catching the blank expression on his face, Coren says, "Wesley or Wes, as you call him, needs us. Especially you, Lawson. He's stumbled upon something that no man was meant to find. And now he's being manipulated to do god-knows-what." Lawson says, "Then you're right. I at least owe it to Wes to try. But you still have some explaining to do."

Coren opens the entrance hatch upward as dirt swirls into the dark hole. "Watch your step." told Coren. Lawson steps on through with the thoughts of Wes on his mind. For him to go this far out of compassion for someone who is like family is a noble gesture to Coren. That remains rare in her eyes. Coren flips on a small switch which illuminates the place fully. "You have electricity? A nomad would give just about anything to have the freedom and ease of light." said Lawson. Coren interrupts, "And why is that, Lawson? Is it to keep the demons away? Or perhaps it is to entertain your children at night with bed time stories?" Lawson defends his position strongly, "No, it's just that where I come from, struggling is a way of life. But as a nomad I've seen a lot of people strive for just the simplest of things." "Have a seat, please, Lawson." Coren said. "I only said that as a kind of 'wake-up,' if you will."

Lawson looks about himself. Beneath the winds and grassy terrain seems to be more like a brick walled basement. This "subterranean get-away" is as ancient and run-down as most areas nomadic people tend to scavenge from. It is filled with artifacts of the past, most of which is tarnished and unrecognizable to Lawson. Most of the items stack the corners and far walls to where he finds an old bench in the center of the room. Behind Coren is a tiny stain glass window that which was somehow carved from out of the cliff's side. Coren moves from the exit-way and walks past Lawson and several other beaten and old benches. There, in a corner lies the strangest and most exotic site to Lawson's eyes.

"Ah, here we are." said Coren as she hunched over the corner. "Do you know what this is, Lawson?" "Some sort of guitar?" he answered. She further adds, "Very good. But it's just not any guitar. It's an electric guitar." She holds it up so Lawson can see it. The guitar is a familiar instrument to Lawson and his people. But this one, with its somewhat clean and vibrant blue finish with a striking red head above its long neck, is completely alien to him. "You see, Lawson, what you nomads and everyone else in this measly world are familiar with are more acoustic in sound." told Coren. Lawson questions, "What powers the lights can also be put into that guitar? How come I haven't heard of such a thing?" She responds, "It goes back to that 'wake-up' call that I'm trying to get around to. And it pertains to your friend, Wes."

Walking across from Lawson, Coren pretends to strum the string-less wonder. She says, "As I've said before: This world just isn't what it used to be. But I suppose nothing is. I wish you could have seen the way things were through my eyes. I miss things, Lawson. Simple things that people took for granted including me. What I wouldn't give to just sit at a small café and order coffee."

THE LEGEND OF COREN

"What are you talking about?" asked Lawson. "And what does that have to do with waking me up to something?" She utters, "You humans are as short-tempered as your little short lives. I'm trying to explain to you that I'm ageless and how I remember things." Lawson takes in a moment to absorb what Coren has said. The boy who imagined more from beyond realizes that he is in the presence of quite possibly a God. He's wide-eyed and speechless to the casually dressed blonde woman that is carrying a sword on her lower back. Along with that guitar, she remains an oddity.

Putting the guitar down on the floor beside Lawson, Coren sits next to him. She seems stressed as she runs her hands through her short hair while leaning over to the floor; avoiding eye-contact. "You're not hungry, are you?" Coren asks. Lawson shakes his head. "Good." she says. "Oh, and please don't ask for my age. It's not just rude but annoying. Well don't look so surprised, Lawson. Say something."

Lawson says, "Thank you for saving me from those desert wolves earlier, Coren. You seem like you have a lot on your mind." "Yeah, you can say that. The one that was trying to kill you earlier, which calls himself, Tomak, may seem mystical but is no God. You see, Lawson, my kind has been around before humanity took its first breath. And ever since then we really mucked things up. My kind has interfered with humanity so much, Lawson . . . There was a time that predates your history when we were first worshiped as Gods. Now it seems as if the more things change the more they stay the same. And I'm not certain what happened to the way things were for humanity but I believe it may have something to do with my kind, given our history and such." "And what about the other Gods, Coren? And were you worshiped before as well?" asked Lawson.

She takes a breather and smiles before telling, "I've always admired humanity. In a sense towards your strengths in nobility, weaknesses through sickness, and curiosities of the beyond, I really did though some might say I was one of the worst Gods around. You see, all those other so-called Gods that are walking the Earth are phonies. The only thing that makes us relatively close to a God is the fact that we cannot die. And our weakness is in our bickering and squabbling over petty things throughout millennia after millennia. As humanity witnesses this they have called us by many names and have made stories and legends up about us. Currently there is one, where you live, about me being a trickster-thief who lore travelers out into the desert to steal from them. Can you believe that? 'All because I was caught 'barrowing' some women shoes. Sorry, I guess I'm just rambling on now. You're not too freaked out about your Gods being a lie, are you?"

Lawson tosses his words back, "I've never really fit in with the rest of the nomads because Wes taught me different. He taught me the importance in thinking for myself. So I'm not really surprised. Just in awe . . . , really. My Mother died when I was young. My Father left our nomadic tribe to find a cure for her illness and never returned. Wes was a controversially smart and brave man who watched over me within our tribe. Then one day he too disappeared from my life, leaving me alone. If he is in danger, then I at least owe it to him to come to his aid. Gods or no Gods, I'll be coming for Wes. So why are we here?"

"Actually I am waiting for someone." Coren explained. Lawson asks, "Is it someone you trust? Someone more like me?" Coren gets up and walks towards the small window. As she looks out and over the valley, she says, "She's more like *me* in some ways. There is more to my kind that you must understand, Lawson. The woman I am waiting on is known by your people as the Oracle. She's gone by many names and truly believes she is a God to this world." "Then she can help us in saving Wes. That is as if she is as powerful as my people believe." Lawson interrupted. Coren snaps back at Lawson in saying, "You're not listening, nomad! We are not granted infinite wisdom or even the right to judge and destroy as we please. No one should be. We've been suffering from madness. I don't know how else to explain what's happening to my kind. The so-called 'Oracle' is a prime example. Just because we have the same colored hair, she believes that we are both Gods from the same blood. And Tomak is just getting worse. For some reason I have been able to 'stay above water.' Except when I'm sleeping, that is."

"Are you talking about your dreams? They can't mean much of anything, Coren." told Lawson in support. She remains silent while keeping her thoughts to herself. Lawson utters, "What happened back there with Tomak? And how did we end up away from the desert sands?" Coren answers, "These black cuffs on my wrists utilize old world technology that you humans created just before the world went sour. Here, let me show you how it works."

With a few presses of her fingers on both cuffs, to Lawson's surprise, an image manifests brightly and silently. While Coren holds her arms close to her chest, the image seems to be coming from one of her cuffs. "Here is the planet Earth as pretty as can be." told Coren. "These cuffs rely on a very old satellite which orbits our planet. I'm not sure on the specifics of how it works exactly but I do know it is military made and somewhat experimental. 'Best way to travel almost anywhere." While Coren turns the power of her cuffs off, Lawson asks honestly, "What's a satellite?" Coren tells, "It's a large man-made object in space that can send and receive information. There's still a lot of junk up there floating around from the past. Some are still sending signals and calling out to our deaf world."

Lawson asks another question, "If what you're saying is true, what happened? And by that I mean what happened to everything? How did things get so bad?" Coren opens up by saying, "Well first you need to understand, Lawson, your own kind in realizing that no matter what state of the world is in, you humans didn't always make things good for yourselves. Just as you may have experienced good and bad times did the people of the past witnessed as well. Like now there was always poverty, famine, disease, war, death, and so on. None of which could ever be truly solved. Now in regards to what happened, my thoughts are a little sketchy. Understand that since it is roughly impossible to kill me, I was put into a limbo-like state by someone I thought I could trust. Finding myself unable to move in a dark chamber I found myself feeling and seeing death countless times. Time was nothing in there as my hallucinations became more real to me. That was my world and I came to except it. Like a depravation chamber, I had a long time to think in there until . . ."

"Until what?" asked Lawson at the edge of his seat. Coren continues, "I can't believe how long it's been since I emerged from captivity. It was one like myself who actually released me. He was strong and powerful. He called himself Matah. 'Matah' laughed as he saved me while telling that it is not every day that Death resurrects a life. From then on the world was a different place to me. A sort of 'madness' seems to have swept my kind, while I'm just getting its lighter affects. I suppose being out of the loop didn't exactly throw me over the hill just yet."

Lawson responds, "I almost can't believe what you're telling me. A world without false Gods. Then what else is truth from fact? What makes the sun rise? What is our meaning and purpose?" "Oh, great! I hope I didn't rupture something in your head, Lawson." Coren said. "'Know this, nomad: There came a time when we were cast out by our human worshippers which began a new dawn and age for humanity. It was as if we had to step aside and make way for their continual growth. Through my eyes, they lived short lives in hopes of a better after-life which my kind could not give them. I believe miracles happen every day. Mankind's survival is one of them. And besides, your old-world-Gods of humanity are still admirable. Just because there are false Gods walking amongst us doesn't mean a true God doesn't exist." "Do you believe in such a God, Coren?" Lawson asked. "Sure, wonderer. Why not? Of course when was the last time *you* went to church?"

Coren is beginning to act impatient as she reveals to Lawson, "I can't believe she isn't here by now. The Oracle is neither here nor anywhere when you need her. I'm afraid I am going to have to go top-side for a bit. Sorry, Lawson, but I shouldn't be very long." As Lawson watches Coren walk over to the old hatch to open it, he utters sarcastically, "That's quite alright. Just leave me alone in here with my small mind on your colossal revelations . . ." And before he knew it, she was gone.

It wasn't long before Lawson yawned deeply. He is beginning to miss home and everything that comes with it like his bed and especially Erika. He lies himself down upon the bench he is sitting on. With what little strength he has in him, Lawson struggles to remain awake. His mind dances with his thoughts on Coren. Lawson, in all his life, has never met such a woman as her. Coren's bravery and sword-wielding showmanship was quite the site for any nomad to see. Stories of masters of weaponry are rarely told these days over adventure and riches. But there appears to be a downside to Lawson's ageless wonder. He realizes that Coren never explained about the danger Wes is in or how he has come to know of him. From anyone's perspective it is as if Coren's mind may be racing a bit; jumping from one subject to another all while knowing their conclusions. One minute, Coren is talking about the past and the next she is giving explanations to the Gods of the Earth. One of which she used to play as. Lawson also remembers Coren telling of madness sweeping over her people. Then perhaps Coren's own madness *is* relative.

As Lawson feels his eyes close, he is beginning to realize how small he is while in the hands of someone who used to be a God. And though small, Lawson may find out if he is as helpless as he seems.

CHAPTER 4

WHILE LAWSON DREAMS, he sees Erika walking through the shadows of his mind. Snow falls from an unseen sky which salts her hair. Lawson can see a tree in the horizon as beautiful as her. And there without notice of Lawson's presence, Erika kneels before it. Lawson begins to walk towards her. He wants nothing more than to be with her at that moment and time. As well, he wants to finally tell Erika how he really feels. She truly made the years together a wonderful experience.

As Lawson approaches closer to Erika, a sudden wind whirls through and in between them. It carries the snow into a blinding flurry that strangely consumes his sweet prize. Lawson shakes his head before yelling her name out to her. Shouting louder and louder, his own words become deaf to his own hearing against the whippings of the wind. That is until Erika is gone from his sight. With his eyes wide in surprise and disappointment, Lawson continues to walk forward until he is underneath the standing tree. The winds have dissipated; leaving nothing more than a long ribbon once tied about Erika's waist that now litters the ground beneath the tree. As the snow continues to fall silently, one would not notice Lawson's body slightly trembling from sadness.

Perhaps he was too late, once again. The opportunity was no more real than the Gods his people worship. He kneels down to where Erika was in place and stares at the slowly drifting ribbon. Lawson thinks to himself about his dark feelings getting the better of himself. He remembers watching his Mother, Sabita's, life draining slowly in her bed. Before Lawson's very eyes, while still beneath the tree, a warm glow emerges just a few feet away. What he sees is a manifestation of a time gone by at his tribe many years ago. There, his Mother lies while surrounded by a young Lawson and his Father, Andolin. Of course Lawson was only 10 years old at the time. He was too young to understand the difficulties of possibly losing Sabita, let alone Andolin.

What Lawson is witnessing begins to turn into bright grains of sand which melts away before his eyes. In its place, sand begins to whirl and form the shape of Erika as a young girl. Being the same age that Lawson lost his Mother, she was a small and frail child; everything he remembered about her physically. Her image walks ghost-like across from his sight and into a black wall of nothing; leaving the dead sands behind.

Once again, Lawson is alone in his thoughts. Or so he thought. He picks up the ribbon which nearly drifted from his grasp. It felt warm as the falling snow melts from its touch. Suddenly, from the corner of his eye, the tree begins to glow a dark and rich, misty color. It is like smoke without fire which consumes its branches until it slithers its way down to the trunk of the tree. There, the mist spreads itself forward and onto the grounds below where Lawson remains kneeling. Finding himself unable to move out of fear, the dark mist moves about and around him; feeling like someone's palms wanting to scratch at his flesh.

Lawson slowly turns his head towards the tree. He can see the snow which is beginning to cease from falling. A voice fills his ears. A deep and dark voice that demands Lawson's attention speaks, "Do not fear, Lawson, for I will be your deliverer and messenger. That, for now, is my purpose to you. You will have to excuse me for the theatrics but I was trying to know and understand you. And Erika . . . she *is* beautiful, yes?" "Who are you?" Lawson spoke up. "And how do you know Erika?"

It speaks again while seeming a little annoyed by Lawson's tone, "I have been called many things, boy. You may call me the Possessor. A simple look through your mind allowed me to see what you have seen and understand your plight. I didn't need to draw my strengths deeply in order to merely reach out to you in your slumber to find the thoughts which keep you up at night. For instance you still starve for your parents though they are more present in your thoughts and heart."

Behind Lawson materializes a tall and shadowy figure. The smog begins to bind itself about the ominous thing tightly. It leers low to Lawson's shoulder and ear; leaving a snake-like tail from behind. "Who are what are you, really?" asked Lawson demandingly. The Possessor speaks more deeply in its new form with one crimson eye opened, "As I have said, I am just a messenger to you, boy. Unfortunately the thing which calls itself, Coren, has unnecessarily planted many seeds within your fertile mind. She will never realize your weak and primitive skull cannot and should not bare the half-truths she has said to you . . . Yet there is an advantage for you, Lawson, within the details. If you could become like Coren, that is to say, God-like, it is possible to raise the dead." "Wha, what are you talking about?" Lawson stutters. What do you mean about being God-like? Like Coren or perhaps Tomak?"

The Possessor moves about and snakes around Lawson's sight. It says in glee, "Easy, boy, easy. You humans are always so predictable in knowing what you want and what you cannot live without. Sabita and Andolin smile upon you, Lawson. They would want what is best for you, child. Though you don't know where your Father lies, you know of where your Mother rests. My message to you is that when you and the pet, Coren, come for me: It is I who can deliver what you truly want."

"But that's impossible. Isn't it? You said that when Coren and I come for you you'll be waiting. You must know about Wes than." told Lawson. The Possessor laughs loudly before saying, "Nothing is impossible, boy. As for Wesley, he is in my utmost care. If it wasn't for his curiosity, I would be like a fish without its water; lifeless and dry. He is dear to me indeed. And such a beautiful and refreshing mind he has. But you do have something to fear in regards to his safety. Another pet, like Coren, believes she can manipulate Wesley and me to do her bidding. Can you believe that? The pets, which turned against their masters, are now making mankind their own pet. What a world this has become."

A voice echoes out to Lawson through the surrounding blackness. The voice catches Lawson's attention. It is Coren speaking as if directly to him but the words just misses Lawson's understanding. "The thing, which calls itself Coren, beckons for its pet." said the Possessor angrily. "Perhaps you should answer." With every word filling the cold air, the tree begins to wither. The smoke slowly begins to recede away from Lawson. And as for the Possessor, it is as if he never existed . . .

While he finds himself alone again, Lawson takes a deep breath in relief. He blinks his eyes just once; long and deeply. While opening them he is face to face with the sweet faced Coren who is in an uncomfortable close proximity with Lawson's eyes.

"Sleep well, Lawson?" Coren asked through a big smile. "Not exactly. I really don't know." said Lawson in a confused tone of voice. Coren moves away from hovering above Lawson and stands closer to her electric guitar. She says, after kneeling down beside him from where he is lying, "While you were sleeping, you appeared a little disturbed and distressed. Now that I think about it, I'm sure my dreams may have brought on the same cues. Can you tell me a little about it?" "Well, Coren," Lawson said before clearing his throat, "I was in an unimaginable place. With snow falling, I first remember seeing Erika. She is a childhood friend from my tribe. Suddenly she was gone and in her place were my memories of my Mother and Father and then . . ."

Coren calms Lawson by placing her palm on his shoulder. She says, "When was the last time a nomad, such as yourself, saw the snow fall? You're doing fine in telling me about your dream, Lawson, but I need to know more. I need to know that my dreams matter and that they're not a part of this rampant madness out there. I need to know that they are not just my old hallucinations from before I was rescued by Matah. Is there anything that is important you can tell me?"

Lawson looks to the gritty ceiling and tells, "I've never personally seen the snow nor felt its cold touch until that dream. I've only heard tales of its vast layers which cover mountains and continents alike. I swear I could literally feel each flake's soft touch on my skin as if it were real. But there was something else. Something that spoke in such a way that you could tell it came from a dark place. From what I remember, it didn't speak too highly of you or your kind. It referred to itself as some sort of messenger. As for you, Coren, you were referenced more than once as a pet. I guess there is something to your dreams after all if any of that sounds familiar to you."

"We have to leave, Lawson." instructed Coren. She moves out towards the sealed hatch in a hurry. "But Coren, wait . . . You have yet to explain your dreams back to me. Are they significant to you? And what about Wes? What danger is he *really* in?" said Lawson as he followed Coren behind. While the blonde oddity makes her way up and onto the surface, she asks directly, "What do you mean by the word 'really?' You're not holding out on me on what you know, are you?" Coren extends her hand out to Lawson who grabs it in delay. "N, no." he answered in a stutter. "It's just that I am growing more concerned for Wes." "Just relax, Lawson." she told. "I'll explain more in time. Right now we have to find the Oracle."

With Coren leading down a passage-way from above the windy scenery towards the valley below, Lawson realizes, from the position of the sun, it is noon. He also realizes that he must have been dreaming for just a few hours. In his nomadic tribe, dreams that seem to reach out and speak to you directly are rare and important. He never thought much of dreams before until he met Coren. She single handedly turned his world upside-down in an instant. Now he doesn't know what to believe. The desert wolves were always one thing but to actually see one turn into part man and beast through what seemed like the spirit of Tomak is simply wrong in nature. But according to Coren, technology from Lawson's human-past can govern the world of today. Which leaves a colossal question: What happened to humanity and its present state? Not even Coren is sure. And it seems as though the people at present have forgotten and moved on for many generations.

Despite everything, Lawson's mind is on the Possessor. What is he? Perhaps the Possessor is as old as time itself. More importantly what does he know about a human, like Lawson, having the ability to become like a God? Could it be possible? With the Possessor's less than fond attitude towards Coren, maybe she truly isn't telling the whole story on what she knows. Yet that doesn't really matter to Lawson because he is with-holding the Possessor's full message: that he can deliver what Lawson truly wants. If the dark creature doesn't know what that is, it is to be a part of a real family again.

They finally make their way down and into the valley. Coren leads Lawson through a thick forest. All of the colors of green catch Lawson's eyes from below to the canopy high. It's a bit quiet except for the sounds of many birds singing out to each other from what seems to be everywhere. The wind remains a constant flow through the tree tops like spirits flying about and around the logs.

"The Oracle," said Coren, "isn't far from here." Further ahead they can hear the slight bustling sounds of a small civilization in a clearing past a few of the wooded trees. A surge of fear from the unknown dwellers constricts Lawson's nomadic spine. He pauses in movement. Lawson's people have endured many hardships and neighboring militant and war-like tribes are one of them.

Coren stops after she can no longer hear Lawson's feet stepping through the brush. "What is it? Don't get shy on me now, Lawson." Coren said impatiently. "Our aid in delivering Wes is straight ahead." Coren knows how to pull Lawson's strings through cunning and intellect. Like a marionette, he proceeds on. Do you always dive in head first, Coren?" Lawson questions. "Or is there strategy to your madness?" Coren is struck by the thought of madness from within her ranks and possibly herself. Though the Oracle believes that she is a God, her strengths can certainly help Coren and Lawson. And of course by strengths, Coren means that quite literally.

"Welcome, Coren. I am pleased that you could finally make it here. Told a tall blonde woman with spry. From Lawson's surprised eyes she is carrying a long and cut tree log on just one of her shoulders. Though terribly beautiful, she has the strength of ten men. Her golden hair cascades down her back while being tied by one large ribbon and a smaller one towards its end. Coren says in an exhausted manner, "Greetings . . . , 'Oracle.' Lawson this is the, well, Oracle. Oracle, meet Lawson. Lawson, Oracle." The Oracle drops down the large tree log roughly. She then composes herself and walks towards Lawson with her palm out. With her more than pretty eyes staring down Lawson, The Oracle says while shaking his hand, "Aren't you cute for a mortal."

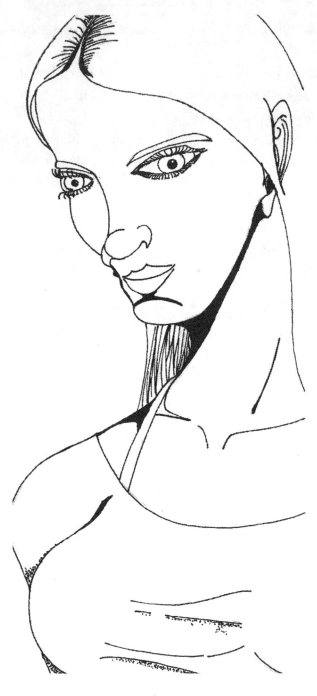

Just after releasing his grip from the Oracle's hand, the people of the small village begin to stop what they are doing and stare at Lawson and Coren. They appear to be a lot like Lawson's tribe. But something in him realizes that these people are very settled and are not much of the traveling type. They have cattle unlike any he has seen before which remain bordered off from the rest of the village by wooden fences. "Come, come, the both of you." ordered the Oracle while grabbing Lawson's hand in lead. Coren tells the Oracle, "Be careful. You'll bruise him. He is important to us."

As they walk further on, Lawson and Coren see that these villagers are indeed very settled in where they live. Fresh fish hang from one stone home's door-less opening. The smell of good food cooking from inside is comparable to the colorful fruits and wild vegetables within baskets outside. Lawson quickly realizes that the stone place must be where the primary cooking is done. The villagers start to go about their business as the three walk farther in. What Lawson finds strange is the fact that the village is full of a few elderly and children of all ages. The youngest of the children are playing while the slightly older ones help around in carrying things with adults as well as tending to the cattle.

While trying to keep up at the pace of the Oracle, Lawson's senses have less time to take in everything. For instance all of their homes are crafted out of stone. He hasn't any time to wonder on how they were made. As for the elderly and numerous children, Lawson can only imagine their suffering that they may have endured in losing any loved ones.

The Oracle stops at the largest and highest stone housing at the end of the village. It has two closed wooden doors as equally impressive as the clean, stone walls that it guards. Coren walks up ahead of Lawson and the Oracle, just before small yet long steps that lead to the thick doors. Her arms are crossed and she doesn't look particularly happy. She opens with a frown, "Do you mind explaining yourself, 'Oracle?' Your task was simple: You were to at least bring one weapon that could help us against Cassie." Lawson immediately questions, "Who is Cassie?" "I don't recall needing permission to help these people or any one. I do as I please, Coren!" explained the Oracle. Coren argues, "Trust me. You're not helping these people in any way, shape, or form! Especially parading yourself as their personal God-savior! Everything is backwards and though everything has gone mad I've learned to deal with it and so can you! You either help *us* or move on!" "Who's Cassie!" yelled Lawson boldly. "Sister, please," the Oracle tells Coren calmly, "the young man wishes for an audience." Coren interrupts, "For the last time I am not kin to you. As for you Lawson, Cassie is what stands in our way between Wes and us. She is also the threat which could set the world back again like what I told you before: A world ruled by my kind. She is also the one who betrayed me and put me in that limbo-like state for many years."

Just as Coren finished speaking, one of the large wooden doors creeks open. The Oracle steps forward and smiles, leaving Lawson and Coren emotionally put off. An older, gray-haired man comes forth from within the shadows of the building. He says, "Once again I thank you, Oracle, for your help in maintaining our village. Is this your friend, Coren and Lawson who you said could further help us in our woes?" The Oracle walks up the stairs and past Coren. She then instructs the two to follow with a wave of her hand. The old man turns in towards the door with a make-shift cane by his side. He says while Lawson and Coren make their way up the stone stairs, "My name is Astor Finn. I reside here in these very holy grounds which this structure was built upon. 'All are welcomed within.'"

Lawson finds the somewhat dark sanctuary gray and drafty. It is mainly kept lit by candle light and glass windows that are too high for Lawson to reach. There are long and wooden benches that allow for more than enough villagers to sit on. Each of them remained in attention to the farthest wall where a stone table-slab lies guarded by candles. Lawson is drawn by the lights ahead and walks slowly between two rows of seating. Astor follows behind while Coren stays behind with the Oracle. Coren remains hot tempered and says to her tall friend in a hush tone, "I can't believe you never showed up. I finally found Lawson and you have nothing that could help us. There is more at stake than helping these people."

The Oracle and Coren have known each other for millennia and beyond. They've always had a good bond. Even through good times, bad times, and worst times, they have made it through on top. But it pains Coren to see her so ill and confused. The Oracle somehow believes she is a God and though given their unique ability to avoid death, the Oracle and Coren's kind are far from it. Coren fears her fate may be the same and she will do anything to prevent losing her mind and who she is.

The Oracle places her palm on Coren's shoulder and brings her head close to her. While looking into Coren's cold eyes the Oracle says, "You'll do the right thing. I know you will."

CHAPTER 5

LAWSON STOPS WALKING just short of the many candles that
lay before the stone slab. He then questions, "What is this place,
Astor Finn?" "Please, call me Astor." he said. "These stone walls,
which surround us, have been known by this village, McLander, as
holy for many generations. Our oldest story is told that a missionary
came to McLander, curing the sick and educating the young and
old in different ways of science and religion. And here, to this day,
we honor that man and what he taught. The village of McLander
wasn't always at peace. Before the missionary came there was
war throughout the lands which isolated our once larger city and
reduced it to a mere village. When he finally came to our village,
there was little to be known about the missionary except that he
taught us how to live without conflict. What he left behind are the
teachings in that very book before you."

Sure enough Lawson sees on the slab a very old book. It hardly
gave any reason to demand his notice. Especially since he has seen
so many from Wes. Lawson imagines that if Wes was with him
Wes would be more intrigued to look through the book's pages.

Wes would want to learn more about the missionary and the villagers' past. He had a way of wanting to see things that were beyond Lawson's comprehension. Though Wes remains captive by another that is like Coren, named Cassie, and at worse in the palms of a dark entity calling itself the Possessor, Lawson could almost feel Wes shadowing him. This gives Lawson the will to continually speak up to the gray and knowledgeable Astor. He asks, "You said that something was troubling your people here, Astor. What could that be?"

Astor says while briefly turning to both Coren and the Oracle's open ears, "If all of you think that you can help us, I'll explain. It was about a week ago when McLander was suddenly visited by someone. Someone I wish I could say was an ordinary man. He called himself the Lord of Death. At first glance he appeared somewhat tall in his suit, tie, and dress pants. The most peculiar thing about him wasn't his taste in clothing but a shroud he kept wrapped below his face. And the only thing he carried was a sheathed sword that he had with a black-coal grip with a diamond tip at its butt-end. I will never forget the day he came."

"What did he want?" Interrupted Coren. She seems sure of herself in Astor's description that it was definitely Matah who visited their village. But for what possible purpose? "Of course after declaring himself as a God, of all sorts, our people rejected him as a fool. He was specifically looking for worshippers and in return offered salvation over death. Ironically he was like the missionary but only taught in himself. He told of many Gods, existing in our world, which are like him. He also spoke of a time coming that will shift humanity." said Astor.

Astor pauses to grip his leg that he supports with his cane. His eyes begin to tell something else about his affliction. "Tell them,

Astor." spoke the Oracle. "Tell them what happened next." Astor opens honestly, "As the keeper of our faith in the missionary's words, I had my fill of the odd visitor's presence. My will was strong in challenging what the so called Lord of Death said and thus told him to leave. Unfortunately, at my age, I hadn't much of a chance to react when he attacked and knocked me down from where I stood which injured my leg. It wasn't long when the strongest of our village stood against he who called himself the Lord of Death. He was so fast. He toyed with the bravest of us and allowed what should have been fatal strikes on his own person to be inflicted. My faith was tested that day on the very ground that I fell upon. I watched, for the first time, a man's wounds heal quickly. The Lord of Death then called himself one name: Matah. It wasn't long after when most of the adults and able-bodied villagers of McLander blindly followed Matah off into the wilderness; leaving behind families and jilted faith."

"Your woes are great." said the Oracle. "But my sister and friend, Coren, is reluctant to assist. She has her own path to follow, unfortunately." Coren remains silent in thought over Matah. Lawson interjects, "It's also true that Coren is righteous in whatever cause she is bound to. Though she *is* helping me, I will certainly ask if she will seek out Matah, Astor." Coren turns her back towards the large two doors and says, "Astor, you have our willingness to assist. I'll see what I can do about Matah but I need some time to think. If it's alright, we'll be here at your village for a while." Coren proceeds to exit out of the sanctuary; briefly filling the drab walls with the outside light. "Thank you, Lawson." told Astor. "Thank you all."

Lawson walks stead-fast in pursuit of Coren. She seems very upset to be helping Astor and the villagers of McLander. Lawson's thoughts are leading to believe that perhaps Matah is too powerful.

As with the Oracle's strength, Tomak's un-natural command of the desert wolves, and Coren's quick sense that can only be matched by her fighting skills, Lawson can only imagine what lies for an immortal who calls himself the Lord of Death.

Outside on the village grounds, Lawson quickly spots the short-blonde-haired Coren walking through McLander. On the steps of the sanctuary he stops to think about what to say or ask Coren in regards to Matah. Thinking is his more-than-human perk. Suddenly a ball rolls towards Coren from a good distance. A young child follows it in pursuit. Coren stops and leans down to pick the ball up. She gazes into the sphere and then at the small child. Eventually she hands the ball off while taking a good look at the serene village.

Lawson approaches her from behind. "I was just thinking metaphorically, that there was a time when I wouldn't have given the ball back." told Coren. "Especially to a human." Lawson says, "Are you talking about how oppressive you and your people were?" Coren answers, "I suppose my people were and still are. Things shouldn't be this complicated. My kind shouldn't be fighting each other. There was a time when we were slaves to more than extreme and oppressive masters. Our old masters were like spirits to this world without a shell or physical body. They had the ability to possess us and gave my people special abilities. And with our powers they made us do horrific things to this world and each other. You would think my kind would learn civility but neither I nor the others did. It was as if our masters' final humiliation was complete. They had already stripped us of who we were and what we were called as a unique people. To them we were only pets suited for torture and fodder for the ground they walked on. But presently I must set things right with my kind.

Lawson walks around and before Coren to tell her, "I had no idea how much weight you've put on your shoulders, Coren. There must be others who can help you amongst your own people, like the Oracle. There must be at least one other, despite the madness, whose shared your past and believes in the peace that can exist with humanity. And those so-called 'spiritual masters' don't hold a chain to you now. You seem to blame yourself for things you have done in the past, as well. I'm sure you've done more than enough good throughout the years. Like saving my life, for instance. And those that . . . possessed you: if you were to confront one today, we would both figure a way to stop it. Or even control it ourselves."

Lawson's mind starts to drift in thought over the promise that the possessor made to him in his last dream. The very thought of being God-like or immortal, like Coren, dances wildly in his head. He comes to the realization that he is keeping that part of his dream from Coren. The Possessor's temptation to make him like Coren so he can see his Mother again over whelms his senses. Coren begins to take notice of his deep thoughts. And though she is not a mind-reader, Coren looks into Lawson's eyes and says, "Thank you for listening, Lawson, and understanding my troubles. Your thoughts are as good as your intentions. I'm sure Erika appreciates that about you." "What? I don't remember telling you about Erika." said Lawson who is dumbfounded. Coren smiles and tells, "Be for-warned, Lawson: My memory is as sharp as my tongue. You mentioned her as your childhood 'friend' while describing your dream to me. Perhaps you'll tell me more about her in the future." Shortly after, the Oracle approaches Lawson and Coren from the sanctuary. She says, "Thank you, Coren. And thank you, Lawson. Your charitable acts will not go un-noticed. So when shall we proceed to face Matah?" Coren looks up at the sky. She knows that the time is against her now to face the Lord of Death. "It's better that we wait until morning. Lawson needs food and water before we can head out. And we can all use a little rest." instructed Coren.

The hours pass steady to what only seems noticeable to Coren. She ate very little while everyone else consumed fresh fish and fruits heartily. With the warm sun setting beyond the forest's edge, she smiled at Lawson who couldn't help himself to a second helping. What is left of the people of McLander are good and honest integrity. They are more than happy to be reunited with their families who have run off into the wilderness with someone claiming to be a God. What the villagers nor Lawson and the Oracle know is that for Coren, facing Matah will be personal.

Coren finishes washing her face over an old sink attached to a wall from within an empty stone house. The water was brought in by a young man from the village. It felt good for Coren to once again travel to another place and settle in amongst people, even if the stay will be short. Coren looks at her reflection through a wall-mounted mirror that seems as old as she is. Though she looks young in appearance, Coren cannot escape her long and deep riddled past. Every scar and wound suffered may heal physically, but emotionally . . . that's a different story.

She suddenly begins thinking about the years that were taken away from her by Cassie; something that was perhaps one of the worst events of the span of Coren's immortal life. She glares at herself, in an emotionally stressful thought, when reminiscing about the last time she saw Cassie standing over her while entombed in a chamber filled with a substance that kept her from moving. Coren clearly remembers how wide-eyed she was when bathed in that very chemical-smelling mixture. She had a fear she has not felt in a very long time when Cassie closed her in that crampt chamber.

And within that darkness, Coren had nothing but time and the unknown.

As Coren now feel the dripping water that ran down her face begin to dry, she moves away from the mirror and sink. Feeling mentally exhausted, the "old woman" walks short of the outside exit and leans against its open post. Her good figure stretches back just a little into the shadows while she crosses her arms about her chest. The well-walked-upon grounds of McLander grow darker by the minute. As the sky dazzles with stars, the sounds of the nocturnal chirp and creep. She watches a more than full and satisfied Lawson talking to the Oracle on the steps of an empty home. The stone place was abandoned by a couple who followed Matah. The villagers are allowing the three to stay there for the night.

Coren can see the two clearly but cannot hear them as their words stay low between themselves. The Oracle stands up and begins walking into the guest home. Lawson is left with a serious look upon his face while still sitting on the step. He then looks up at the night sky as he has done countless times before. Coren thinks to herself that God only knows what he and the Oracle have talked about. Like Coren, the Oracle, though more confused, is still like an ocean when it comes to past history and knowledge on almost anything. "Are you alright, Lawson?" asked Coren. She walks from the door-less post towards Lawson who doesn't keep his eyes away from the heavens. "The Oracle was just telling me about my history," said Lawson, "and what happened to humanity." Coren is stunned and tells Lawson, "She told you what? I'm sure it's what she tried to tell me once when I was searching or, should I say, putting the pieces together of what I've missed for so many years."

"I understand that, Coren," explained Lawson, "but you were gone for a very long time. To you, the Oracle may seem off-put in her beliefs that there is more to her than you give credit for." "Go ahead, Lawson," Coren says impatiently, "and explain to me what she told you." Lawson takes a deep breath before saying, "There was a war in a period of time in which our world has reached its peak. The Oracle tried her best for me to comprehend such a thing. Everything had its place as people, though many had enough, still starved for more. Eventually the world led to one thing: Power. She also explained how their remained a race for stronger and more powerful weapons in the skies and heavens themselves. To add to the confusion, it was as if the world shrunk overnight as many foreign industries neighbored in each other's back yards with a new technology that allowed the world to be as one. It was a false hope, she further explained, after the 'darkness' came. Somehow that technology went black for a while which allowed the wilderness to settle amongst the newly divided lands. Strangely enough, as powers from the West explored the farthest reaches from beyond our planet, that's when the war washed over like a great flood. But it was a conflict unlike any imagined in our time now. A new chemical-disease came with it as death followed all around. With most of humanity gone, by a number I cannot understand, most were able to flee this world and were never seen again. I am a descendant of that chaos. I realize now that in my family's past that for some reason they were left behind in which they chose later to be nomads."

"Yeah, same old crazy story by the Oracle." said Coren. Lawson adds, "It's fine, Coren. I can except humanity's mistakes and be at peace with what they have done." "Why?" Coren asks. "I do remember this planet being more beautiful and somewhat tolerant for me many years ago. How come you're so easy to forgive?" "Because," Lawson said frankly. "They are all still my people."

Coren says, "I'm sorry Lawson but I can't believe in such fairy tales told by the Oracle. War and disease may be something but what's left of humanity flying off into space to never be seen again is all too much for me." Silence between Lawson and Coren begins to fill the air. Coren opens up again by saying, "It's okay to cling to what gives you comfort. Believe in what you want, nomad, because life is too short." Lawson gives out a comforting smile to the ageless wonder's careless comment. It finally occurs to Coren what she said as she joins in with a grin of her own and says, "'Very funny. I'm very aware of my immortality. Just don't ask for my age, like I told you before."

"It's getting late." said Lawson. As they turn and walk into the house, Coren says, "Another day is upon us. If only you could step into my shoes, Lawson, and understand what that really means to me."

The Legend of Coren

CHAPTER 6

Within the cozy yet dim stone walls of the abandoned home in McLander, Coren lies on her side on a hand-made mattress. She previously watched Lawson dose off first which was followed by the Oracle. Coren finds it rather odd that Lawson is comfortable enough to gather any rest over someone whose mind has shifted towards "deeper waters." Mortals have always fascinated her. Coren has remained as still and quiet as possible so as to not disturb them. She fails to realize how tired she has become as the "dark blanket of slumber" slowly rolls over her gently.

But Coren continues to watch on as Lawson sleeps deeply. How innocent he is, she thinks, and calm about everything he has seen. To Coren, he is as every bit a sweet young man as he can be. Unfortunately, she may never know the bitter sweet secret he holds. She thinks that perhaps Lawson's calm is because of the comforts of home and being surrounded by other people as contributing factors. And it has been a while since Coren has been able to lie in a bed. Humanity has its benefits as Coren realizes that may be they would be better off without knowing the existence of her kind. But it is too late for that. Humanity has always wondered about vast things beyond their comprehension and while creating many tools from their "blessed pool." Unfortunately they didn't or couldn't construct a means of traveling through time. Ironically, she feels she is stuck in the past and unable to move forward. Her memories remain as distasteful as ever while haunting her about some of the good times spent.

The world has been lost to her and is no longer recognizable through her Westernized eyes. Coren's friend, who now calls herself, the Oracle, has been watched through those same eyes to only choke and drown slowly into madness. All the while, Cassie, her betrayer, has resurfaced to only cause more grief than good. But before she can face her, Coren must see to it that the people of McLander do not follow in worshipping Matah. It's like she is standing against the wind while alone with just her short-sword in hand. As she watches Lawson slowly turning in his bed, a glimmer of hope crosses her bleak thoughts. She isn't quite alone after all.

With her eyes drawing down into the dark recesses of her mind, she can swear that the temperature has dropped. Interestingly enough, she remains still as Coren wishes to keep Lawson and the Oracle undisturbed. Ever so still she remains as the gray walls seem to fade into nothing.

Snow is falling all around Coren as she finds herself walking through its calm and brushing flakes. The sky is like a blank canvas though she doesn't care to see. Over a thousand times Coren has walked this imaginary path. But she *is* tempted to look down and about herself in notice of a long and beautiful kimono dress that she is wearing. The dreamscape is as always inescapable as she continues to walk towards a small hut in the distance. While squinting, Coren can barely see through the lovely yet vexing snow.

As the snow-covered-hairs of Coren approaches the hut, she can clearly see that the place is very old. It was made with dried mud for mortar. She hasn't seen something this old since humanities early beginnings. Seeing the snow blanketing its round roof, Coren begins to wonder on why it is here now. The temperature can be felt dropping which causes Coren to hug herself.

"Kasin?" called out a young man from the interior of the hut. Coren is completely taken by surprise. She literally takes a step back and in a puff of a cloud of frosty smoke from her breath she utters, "It can't be . . ." It's a name from a language she hasn't heard in thousands of years. In his native tongue the young man speaks again, "Kasin, I know it's you out there. Come in and warm yourself up by the fire, will you?" Like a moth to the flame, Coren is drawn closer to the familiarities of the hut and the person's voice who called out to her by the name, Kasin. Kasin, as Coren remembers, is just one of many names she used to go by. The name is so old that it is one she nearly forgot about. Who else could possibly know that name? Coren isn't always particularly proud of her past in regards to the time she was known simply as Kasin.

Coren comes to the hut's small and quaint entrance. She opens its thinly laced wooden door. Coren didn't want to reveal her vulnerabilities in regards to not knowing if he is a friend or foe so she creeps in silently. Her sense of smell flares to fresh fish cooking on a spit over a fire at the far end of the room. She closes her eyes once just to reopen them slowly to the rustic scene. Where there is no iron or metal things; clay pottery, plates, and baskets made from straw by hands exist within the simple hut. No evidence of any higher technology can be found here. The architecture of the hut didn't even allow another room to be present as Coren notices two sleeping bed-rolls made of animal fur lying flat in a corner. The hut's dull and gray colored rusty brown interior comes to life with green vines creeping from around the doorway.

Suddenly, Coren sees the head of a shadowy figure turn slightly; seeing her from the corner of his eye. She fully notices him now. His back is turned in a sitting position towards the small and warm fire. He turns his head away from Coren and watches the fish eagerly as they cook. "I am glad you are back and here with me, Kasin." he said. "Did you get the things we need for this food?" Coren's heart skips a beat as she realizes where she is and who the mysterious person must be. He's wearing thick wooly clothes, although he is close to the only warmth in the room. Coren remembers how the winters were here in this very hut. The bed-rolls also bring forth strong cognitive feelings. She remembers sleeping close to the young man as he shivered through many nights. It was as if he needed her warm embrace which she gave every time without delay. He was her first love.

"Jalil," Coren calls out softly, "what is this?" "You've been away, Kasin, for almost half of the sun's rise," told Jalil, "so I began cooking already." Jalil continues to watch the ambers burn and flicker. Coren couldn't bring herself to move any further within the small hut. It is as if her feet are glued to the rough floor. Could it really be Jalil after all this time? Coren doubts herself as she prays for anyone at any time to be someone other than Jalil. "You can't be here, Jalil. You can't still be . . ." Coren said as if to defy the very will of fate itself. "Of course I am, 'funny-face.' Because of you I'm here." A silence brews forth to only be interrupted by the wind outside which shutters the entrance door. Jalil can be heard coughing low which becomes louder and deeper. Coren reaches her arm out towards his direction. Her lips murmur his name, "Jalil." She wants nothing more at this moment than to hold him again and keep him safe with her forever.

Coren, like most of her kind, were a scourge to the land and the human race. After they banished their dark and shell-less masters they were free to do as they pleased. As for Coren, also known as Kasin, her destruction knew no bounds. Presently her guilt would have broken the average man. It was after she and many of her kind came to a settlement that was destined to be a great city in the making, did they demand the populace there to worship them. With the people contributing as their slaves, Kasin and her kind hoped to start an empirical dynasty where they would gather and make a name for themselves. That's when one man stood where many did not. His name was Jalil. He was the son of a powerful healer in the region. That gave him weight amongst his people who allowed him to be their voice.

Kasin began to admire Jalil over time as it was his nobility and wit which saved his and many of his people's lives from the cruelties of enslavement. But what Kasin hoped to be a utopia and a new era for her people would crumble when her kind began to strife over petty and materialistic things. And governing a community without official laws for her people was hard enough as the threat of a sudden human population growth loomed as many began to question them as Gods. A human rebellion was at hand as the power went to the strongest of the "Gods" while the weaker, much like Kasin, were handed what was left. Though the shift in power was abrupt, it was the weaker that had the strength in numbers. Lines were drawn with people caught in the middle.

Yet from Kasin's higher perspective on what was happening, she couldn't help but think about Jalil. He had family and friends who she helped to make into slaves. It dawned on her that she was no different than a slave master. The whip was passed down to her. Before the small city was destroyed by Kasin's kind in their ignorant and rampant melee, she freed Jalil. It was too late for the others as Kasin knew that she could only save him. They ran together and lived on the outskirts of the world.

The two would end up spending their last days together in that very hut that Kasin, who now calls herself Coren, finds herself in. She finally gets the courage to move forward from her ill conscious thoughts that held her to the floor. Coren throws her arms around Jalil as if panic stricken. While tears begin to roll down her cheeks she says, "I'm sorry. I'm sorry for what I've done to this world and you."

Coren closes her eyes and embraces Jalil harder. She can feel a sudden wisp of what seems like thick sand caving in to where she is holding Jalil. While opening her eyes, the color of Jalil changed to a gray and dull exterior. He didn't move which prompted Coren to call out his name, "Jalil." She places both palms onto his grainy back. Coren watches horrified as her hands sink deep and through the other side of his chest. When she swiftly pulled both of her arms out, Jalil's head, which was also sand, sifts down and falls into a puddle of itself where his body pummels to the floor and into nothing. Coren is shaken and is only left with Jalil's sandy dust which streams through her hands.

She stands tall and doesn't bother wiping the tears from her wet face. She feels numb from perhaps all the years of torment of witnessing death. Infact it was one of Matah's philosophies which state that because their kind could not die, then perhaps they were never alive to begin with. It was from there that Coren felt strongly that humans shouldn't be with them in any way. And as Coren continues to stare at the pile of sand made from Jalil, she walks back until she is out of the hut's door.

"You don't truly believe that, do you Kasin?" questioned the voice from a woman. "You?!" bellowed Coren. "But why?! Why him?! Why Jalil?!" Coren turns her head towards the snow-filled path she made earlier to find a woman standing near a fruitful tree. She is tall and full figured while wearing a thick and cozy striped kimono. Coren trudges her buried feet towards the woman who in turn looks back to pick an apple from the tree; showing that the woman's short hair is pushed back into a small bun. Coren hasn't seen this woman before but knows what she is. "'Care for one?" the tall woman asks as she motions to hand Coren the picked apple. "This one is especially sweet."

Coren stares at her reflection on the blood-red apple and says calmly, "I know what you are." The woman curls the apple back towards her and takes a solid and firm bite. "Do you now, Kasin?" she says as if pleasingly entertained. "Or should I call you Coren . . . , *now*." Coren balls her fists and says harshly, "You are one of many that go by many names. You and your kind have enslaved countless others like me while stripping us bare of who we are. Your kind is the lie which never ends. And now you call yourself the Possessor because you have no shell!" "Watch your tongue, pet!" spoke the Possessor. "For it was I who delved deep into your psyche to find what changed you so long ago. Jalil can still be with you, Coren, forever. That is if you free me from my dark prison. The thing which calls itself Cassie will be no match for the both of us once I am free."

"And what about Wesley?" asked Coren through her teeth. "Ah, yes. The young man's guardian is only a mere bargaining tool. I am especially sure that Lawson will be pleased to be reunited with family." Coren takes a moment for things to sink into perspective. She stared into this demon's eyes before thousands of years ago and won. With the help of her people, those like the possessor were banished and buried deep into the darkest recesses and crevices of the world. Unable to be destroyed, the Possessor found a way to reach and scavenge out the minds of others. And being in such depredation only increased its power.

Coren turns her back in deep thought. The Possessor begins to feel every spark of delectable brain-matter surging from one end of her mind to the other. It knows her inner thoughts which are surfacing around helping Lawson by defeating Cassie. The Possessor knows now that Coren, though driven by a desire for revenge, is in doubt of her ability to defeat or even reason with the immortal Cassie. Coren's temptation by the Possessor makes her cringe. She reminisces again on the crimes of nature that were forced upon her by his evil kind.

The Possessor speaks, "The temptation and the allure of power, Coren, is what I am truly guilty of. I create and give promises which are kept. That dress, this place, and Jalil can all be real. I know of which you crave. It's all so predictable in regards of those with hearts to have. Jalil was human but here he can be so much more, like you. Jalil will not die alone again."

In a fit of rage and emotions, Coren turns around and belts out, "I was there when Jalil passed through the cold night as I held him as always. He caught a bitter illness from which he didn't wake from. He didn't die alone. No human does! What you're truly guilty of is twisting, distorting, and taking advantage of the emotions of others. You have no right, no right to use his name in vein!"

As the falling snow intensifies, it is as if a line was "drawn in the sand." The Possessor drops the once bitten apple onto the ground; finding itself buried deep in the snow. The Possessor stares deeply into Coren's eyes as Coren stares back with her eyes in hatred.

Coren can see that the Possessor isn't impressed. In fact the shell-less creature has a cold and blank stare as it is intentionally reading Coren's fiery mind. "You would like nothing more than to twist and throttle my being," told the Possessor, "and to burn and destroy me as you once did the world as Kasin? Bravo. You're learning to be what you truly are. You see, no matter how you and your kind try and hide what you are neither of you will be like them. You will never be human. You and your kind are an inconceivable mistake that which are worse than pets! You've called yourselves humanity's Gods?! Your kind have drank their blood in the morning, broke bread with them in the afternoon, and loved them in the evening!! And you, Coren, are a plague amongst the 'human disease' which must be eradicated!!!"

The Possessor swiftly motions its arm in a hostile manner and swipes the air with a closed fist towards Coren's head. Coren reacts faster as if time had slowed down. Her ability to move and see things faster with just her two eyes is her immortal trait as she is able to catch the blow with her arm and deflect as a follow through with such. Coren is keeping a cool and solid head on her shoulders as she engages defensively from the Possessor's continual assault. The Possessor focuses on trying to land a blow on Coren's face by flailing its arms left from right. The combative moves continue as the dark entity leans its torso closer to Coren; stretching lean muscle from fat. Coren reacts by holding her ground and changing her stance while twisting her torso on a swivel. But the stronger Possessor whirls its leg up high to Coren's face which just nearly misses her by a hair. The Possessor than seizes an opportunity to strike Coren's mid-section with both closed palms after swiftly bringing its leg down.

It was as if a burst of air had cut between the both of them when Coren sailed further away. Yet her feet managed to skid and gain traction on the ground from beneath the snow. Coren takes in a moment to think. She knows that the Possessor can read her thoughts. But it is those very thoughts that fuel her. They are what begin to pump and move her legs towards the Possessor steady and now fast. Coren fully engages in fighting the shell-less entity while thinking of Wesley, Lawson, the Oracle and Jalil. Coren lands a solid crossing punch across the Possessor's face. She follows quickly with another cross-attempt with her other arm coming close to her face until it was blocked and pushed away. Coren returns with a long and risky back kick after swinging her torso in the opposite direction. She wasn't sure if she landed a strike as the Possessor seemed to float further from combat like a leaf in the wind. But Coren moves in further; driven by fear of what havoc this creature has already caused.

The Possessor stands its ground firmly and in a surprise begins to manipulate the wind with its arm and hand gesturing. The air's mere cold touch slams into Coren's abdomen and face. "This world is mine to control!" bellowed the Possessor. "Your mind is my subject to do as I please." Coren holds her beaten body with one arm as she slowly steps through the snow. By raising both arms, the Possessor once again manipulates and turns the air into hard yet invisible matter far above Coren. The Possessor brings its feminine arms down towards Coren's direction harshly. The augmented air smashes into Coren like a ton of bricks. She collapses under the weight which dissipates like the air of which it is.

Something can be heard low from under the breath of Coren. She didn't move but spoke quietly which prompted the Possessor to walk closer towards Coren. Feeling dissatisfied, the Possessor places both hands on its hips and slightly nudges over Coren with its shoe enough so as to see the defeat on her face. The Possessor is in shock to see Coren smiling. Though it is a small smile, it suggests mockery and anything but a humiliating end to one's self. Her mind spurs a lack of fight in this somewhat non-existent world created by the Possessor. What Coren thinks mostly about is Jalil and how Lawson reminds her of him. But deeply, Coren keeps in mind of what the Possessor really is. "You're pathetic." mocked Coren. "You and your whole species or whatever you things are have lost this world."

"What?!" yelled the Possessor. With its large humanoid eyes in disgust it grabs Coren off of the cold ground. The Possessor brings her face to face with Coren. Coren says honestly, "We buried you for countless generations and your only response when making contact with the outside are false promises to save your weak and shell-less hide. I don't have to be a mind reader to know that you are hopeless and sad as you are arrogant and foolish."

Coren continues to boldly stare through the womanly image of the Possessor's face which frowns in such a dark way. So much so that it would make the most hardened man cringe. In fact, Coren expects the Possessor to be at its worst and most violent towards her while she feels weak from the previous assault. But oddly, the Possessor did nothing of the sort. Instead it released Coren as its finger-tips became like a dark and somewhat transparent fog. The fog begins to quickly consume down both of its arms like fire to paper but without any burning. All that remains of the Possessor now is a dark and fireless smoke which evaporates into the air like nothing.

Coren slowly gets up and looks on to notice that the snow has stopped falling. She walks with clear thoughts on the consequences of trusting the Possessor. And though she is blind in not knowing her future, she knows that the Possessor must not go free from its prison.

The Legend of Coren

—————————— •❦• ——————————

CHAPTER 7

COREN AWAKENS A little shaken with her mind spinning. But she is confident in getting things done for the day. The name, Jalil, echoes through the recesses of what is left of the dream she had last night. 'Just a "scar" left behind by the sandman, she thinks to herself. As she moves from off of the welcoming mattress, Coren notices that both Lawson and the Oracle are gone from their beds. She slowly brushes bits of her hair from her face and eyes and calls out, "Lawson!"

"Over here, Coren." told Lawson from outside. Coren walks through the stone housing and towards the exit. She finds Lawson playing with a ball amongst some of the other children in the village. He is using just his feet like a game that Coren remembers from many years past. The young-ones are cheering and laughing at Lawson's expertise. Not a single one is without a smile from ear to ear. Coren is eventually caught with the same expression by Lawson who loses his step and falls to the ground.

Coren steps down from the stoop of the stone housing to try and assist Lawson from off of the ground. But instead, Lawson's pride is able to get up to dust his self properly. "Did you sleep well, Coren?" asked Lawson. Coren answers in a serious tone, "Not exactly. There is more to my dreams that I must explain to you and the Oracle. Where is she, anyway?" "The Oracle is there," answered Lawson, "by Astor. They've been talking for a while since you were sleeping in." Further up ahead is indeed the Oracle who is conversing with Astor. Astor is standing on the steps of McLander's holy sanctuary. Coren quickly walks up to them as words about Matah are being thrown around.

The Oracle tells Astor, "Matah will not get away with what he's done to you and your village. With Coren by my side I am confident that we'll bring back McLander's people." Astor nods his head to agree but says in doubt, "Matah didn't force anyone to go with him in worship. I fear that convincing the people otherwise will be as hard a challenge as the Lord of Death himself. Whatever you and your friends can do will be very much appreciated." Astor walks into the sanctuary with a heavy heart. The Oracle then realizes that Coren is beside her. The both of them have been friends for quite some time and during those periods of chances met on this world; they have encountered many of their own. Together they have won and outsmarted those foolish enough to go against them.

"Though change is inescapable and surprising, it's always the same, eh, Coren?" told the Oracle. Getting right down to business, Coren asks, "Did Astor say anything else in regards to Matah? I'd like to get this over with as soon as possible." The Oracle stares at Coren in worry about her belligerent nature surfacing. "Relax, Coren. Astor told me everything I need to know about Matah, including his whereabouts. Are you okay? You look a little disheveled." said the Oracle. Coren says loudly, "Disheveled?! You should look in a mirror, old friend! I know I have my issues, which are more real than I've expected, but I don't need your comments at this moment."

"Whoa, whoa!" yelled Lawson who walks steadfast to Coren and the Oracle. "There's no need for that. I'm sure the Oracle means no harm here. And Coren: You were saying something about your dreams that you mean to tell the Oracle and me?" Coren gives out a long and deep huff. She is almost lost in what she wants to convey. What she wants to bring up about her dreamscape last night reflects some things, like Jalil, which are personal to her. But that only reminds Coren of the very real danger that the Possessor has. Coren must warn Lawson and the Oracle.

Coren says, "It was the Possessor, last night, who came to me in my dream in the image of a woman. The Possessor, as Lawson knows from his own dreams, is one of the disembodied masters that you remember, Oracle, from our past that we have banished into the depths of this world. But this one is apparently more powerful than before and I'm not exactly sure how that can be." The Oracle questions, "It can't be true? But if you're sure than there is nothing we can do for this world. I almost cannot believe that we are being toyed with by one of those things again. But I thought that we were over and past that chapter of our lives? I suppose it is just the curse of eternity we have, Coren."

Coren can see that the Oracle is visibly shaken over the once enslavement and brutality of the Possessor's kind which was so long ago. Their monsters' scars can still be felt on every immortal that is like Coren and the Oracle. But for mortals like Lawson, he couldn't possibly understand the threat of having the Possessor reach out to him. Coren says honestly, "Maybe you're right, Oracle. And furthermore it has also found its claws around Lawson. I know from my last dream that this Possessor favors in temptation and desire.

It made everything so real and so wanting. The very thought surges through my being. As for Lawson, he hasn't confessed to me, if any, what the Possessor may have said to him in desire."

Both Coren and the Oracle stare at Lawson while waiting for an answer in response. Lawson is completely caught off guard. He knows that he should tell Coren the truth about his own personal dream and temptation. But Lawson can feel an embrace by the Possessor like a warm and soothing hug by his Mother, Sabita. So instead Lawson told her something which he himself didn't know that would drive a stake through Coren's heart when questioned. He asks Coren, "Since you say he tempted you also, what is *your* desire, Coren?" Coren is taken back to Jalil but doesn't say anything at first. Her sweet mortal Jalil wasn't some person meant to be forgotten. But it is Coren's solid pride that keeps her from sharing his memory at bay.

It is not realized by Coren that her so-called pride is a mere tool of fear. Perhaps it is in not wanting anyone or thing using such information to do harm to her. Or maybe it is simply the fear which makes her build walls around others while only showing her quick-to-fight nature. Yet in a world of madness, where creatures lurk in hidden corners of the hemisphere and human-like super-beings vie for dominance, is a good reason for Coren to remain "anti-social."

"Let's just say that the Possessor cut through my psyche deep." explained Coren. "It found a way to read my thoughts and exploit that fact. I have nothing more to say about that." The Oracle tries to understand what her friend is saying. But they have lived too many lifetimes to figure it out. The Oracle places her palm on Coren's shoulder and says, "We should head out now." Coren turns to her charcoal-black wrist-cuffs and brings up a digital holographic display of their current location. The village of McLander is dwarfed

TERRY LEE SMITH JR.

in comparison to the wilds of forestry which have overgrown beyond where they are standing.

"Coren, where-ever did you get such a device?" asked the Oracle. Coren tells, "It was 'borrowed' from Tomak. Unfortunately the power is always low and takes time to self-charge." The Oracle reveals, "Astor explained to me that Matah is east of here in a place that they refer to as the Dead Ruins." Coren says bluntly, "Let me guess: it's over here, right? Leave it to the Lord of Death to be so dramatic." Coren brings about and enhances the so-called Dead Ruins for everyone to see. It is an oddity of ruined buildings, spires and rubble from a once pre-modern resort that overlooks the back drop of a dried water fall. From below the dried and thirsty fall lies a ghost ship in ruin. The large vessel remains drier than Lawson's own backyard: The Center of the World.

They begin to walk towards the outer perimeter of the village with Coren leading the way. "Sometimes it's like I have to shake or 'ding' these cuffs, you know." Coren said while waving her arms strongly out in front of herself. "Or otherwise it takes long for it to work." "Don't worry. You don't look that ridiculous." told the Oracle. Lawson interjects, "Yeah, Coren. And besides, we're just about away from everyone else's attention at McLander." "Very funny, you two." told Coren sharply. A flash emits directly in front of Coren. "That's it. It's beginning to work." said Coren. "Fools go first to favor the bold."

As a swirling portal emerges and begins to expand, the Oracle says, "Wait, Coren. Astor also warned me about our destination being treacherous. He said that the Dead Ruins is a place that no traveler, bandit or fool has dared to go. The area is considered unstable. I've been thinking that this may not have been safe for the villagers who followed Matah and . . ." "Then we should hurry." Coren said undeterred by the Oracle's less than spirited words. "Matah must be convinced otherwise to let the villagers follow a more truthful path." While realizing that the portal is unpredictable, Coren gestures for both Lawson and the Oracle to step through.

Walking within, they find themselves on the other side of the "doorway." Coren, Lawson, and the Oracle can see what looks like a very tall tower; stretching and narrowing high into the air. The tower, once metallic and now very rusty, looks as if it was a part of something even larger than what still stands. This magnificent "monument," which captures their attention and captivates their souls, is like the long deceased skeletal remains of a giant that was once birthed by man. Feeling the urge to walk ahead of the pack, Coren utters, "Man's ideals of a better place for a better tomorrow." "What?" asked Lawson. The Oracle answers for Coren, "I believe this place was once a resort for vacationers. Now it's ruined, dead, and gone. Like everything else, I suppose." Lawson asks innocently, "What's a resort?"

The nomad, Lawson, lacks most knowledge of his past and who he is and how great humanity once was. For what it's worth, humanity's peak "season" was impressive. From wrist cuffs that can open pathways to almost anywhere on the planet to wondrous cities that stretch high in the clouds above. But as seasons change, things have a way of remaining at present.

The Oracle walks on from behind Coren who continues her own steady path further in to the Dead Ruins. Lawson seems to be the only one hesitating to find Matah and the foolhardy, missing villagers. But this mortal-man knows what must be done about helping the villagers of McLander. Their families, or better said, no family should be torn away. So Lawson bites his tongue and sees past what may lie ahead to where he can see Wes. Walking beside Coren now, Lawson's ears miss her saying, "I don't know what's ahead but I especially need you to be cautious, Lawson." Lawson's mind is on seeing Wes again and ultimately his Mother. "Hmm?" squeaked Lawson. It's good that Lawson has Coren who has a strong interest in helping him out. Lawson grins at Coren while thinking of her good natured quality to put a fist to what is right.

Coren lightly smacks Lawson on the side of his head. "What was that for?!" asked Lawson loudly. Coren replies, "Haven't you been listening to me? I was telling you to halt." If not for Coren, Lawson would surely be lost. Ahead, they find themselves on top of a large hill that leads down to overgrown flora, bushes and trees. "Matah should be down and through there." said the Oracle. "How can you be sure?" asked Lawson who is still rubbing the side of his head. Coren simply replies, "Just look up and ahead. There are more towers and spires that can be seen farther out; stretching skyward. If he truly believes he is a God, than that is where he'll try to dramatically convince his followers."

Though the hillside is somewhat steep, there is still a path that they can follow which was made by the indigenous animals that venture there. Naturally, Coren leads ahead, but slower and more carefully. Lawson says to Coren, "There is much I still don't understand about the madness being so rampant amongst others like Matah. Is it that everyone's affected; human and your kind alike? Or is it just randomly at a time?" Thinking before she speaks, Coren's mind drifts back to the Possessor, from last night, and answers, "The Possessor has become so much more powerful than I could imagine . . . But at least I have an answer to my dreams: It's the Possessor's doings. The madness that has spread *is* caused by that monster. Yet it only leaves me with more questions. The

Possessor is only one of many banished away. Could it be that the ill will of others, like Matah, is because of another shell-less creature that was cast down and away from another corner of the world?"

Lawson can sense that Coren is upset. He can never truly realize the traumatic lives she has lived through out millennia after millennia. It wasn't just Jalil she keeps to herself. It's also who she was in a time when humanity was at its most vulnerable. Before the atrocious self-proclaiming-Gods of Earth, like the Possessor, were cast down into pits, oceans and such, they stripped their "pets," like Coren, of their beginnings and what they were. The spiritual beasts' influenced only in pain, suffering, war, self-indulgence, and ignorance. Those are what carried on from Coren and her kind when they set forth on to the world of men and women without the chains of slavery. And with such new powers amongst humanity; they were destined to crush and rule. Legends of their staples in life soon became mostly myths. Like a child who was treated like a beaten dog, that world was once all Coren knew.

That is until she met Jalil. Jalil didn't have to tame Coren or destroy her or even burry her into the deepest and darkest crevices of the earth. But rather unthinkable to Jalil and unfathomable to Coren, he stole her heart. Then, Coren did not know she had a heart to take. As time with Jalil came and went, she discovered empathy, compassion, love, and justice for other humans and those like herself.

The Oracle steps forth as each of them come down from the hillside and are confronted by the thick flora. "I'll go first." said the Oracle. Making their way through the claustrophobic weeds and tall tree trunks that are close together, the Oracle moves aside a fallen and rotten branch that is as thick and tall as Lawson and Coren combined. The Oracle tosses the useless branch to the side like a feathered pillow which smashes loudly into pieces farther away. "Let's keep it quiet." Coren scolded in a hushed tone of voice. Lawson couldn't help but notice the canopy of the trees. It is eerily silent enough, where they are trudging through, but the tree tops are busy with life. As a nomad, he rarely sees so much of anything but the Center of the World and its inhabitants. To Lawson, the dimensions of the trees paint the most alien picture. He is almost lost at what vistas Coren has shown him recently. That is until Coren says, "We're almost there at the Dead Ruins. Oracle, what do you see?" The Oracle doesn't say anything. In fact she remains as silent as the green surroundings they find themselves in.

Coren and Lawson can finally see the Dead Ruins for themselves as they push away tall weeds from their sight. The area is massive with decayed structures narrowing high into the sky. The salted and circular grounds have only scattered and wild shrubbery. Coren knows that this is an awful and bleak place to lead any of McLander's villagers to. From contrast, McLander is an oasis to this very arid, dead, and rugged place. It doesn't make sense for Matah to do what he has done. While stepping out of the brush, Coren asks out loud, "What could you really be up to, Matah? Why are you acting this way? I thought I understood and had a handle on the madness..."

The three begin walking deeper into the ruins. They are cautious of the tall and ghostly spires and what may lie behind the larger and more grounded rubble. "Where do you think they are, Coren?" asked the Oracle. The baron scenery doesn't show any signs of life from any which way that they can see. But there is one place they haven't looked: Over the dried waterfall. As Coren leads Lawson and the Oracle to the rugged edge, they can see what looks like very old construction materials. Lawson, as an avid nomadic scavenger, has seen many of these things before but has never known their appropriate names. "Careful, Lawson, the edge is just beyond that dozer." told Coren while watching Lawson walking through the rubble. "Dozer? What a strange name for such a big and ugly old thing. Then I suppose you know what this is too?" Lawson said before picking up an old metal object. "That's a wrench, sweetheart." Coren explains simply.

Lawson tosses the wrench over the edge. Immediately they hear the wrench make a loud sound of impact which they expected to fall for a while over and into the dried bed. Coren walks fast to peer around the decayed dozer. What she sees are wooden steps with wire railings for support that lead down the side of the cliff. Coren boldly steps forward to see if it is safe and stable. "Let's go. They must have gone this way down." said Coren. She carefully leads the Oracle and Lawson as the wooden stairs remain surprisingly stable amongst the environmental changes over time.

Shortly they reach the bottom to where the stairs end onto a platform. There, they can see that the cliff's side has two sets of very large windows with a closed door in between them. The windows are caked with dirt and dried mud. Though Coren cannot see what's inside that doesn't stop her from proceeding towards the door. Her intentions are clear and that is to convince Matah to allow the people, who are following him in worship, to think for themselves. Matah is no God and for Coren to allow the thought of bringing the Earth back to a time when they walked over and enslaved mankind is unacceptable. For the innocents who rest, like Jalil, and those who struggle now, Coren feels obligated to slow Matah in his tracks.

Coren begins to open the door slowly before a gust of wind inadvertently flushes through the doorway; slamming the door inward. Her eyes slowly adjust to the dark interior in contrast to the bright and sunny outside. "Matah!" yelled Coren. She can see the shadowy heads of others quickly turn while showing the whites of their eyes. Coren grips her sword's handle tightly. She is still trying to take everything that lies within. The shadowed people must be the villagers since they are numerous. They appear gaunt and weak and to the sight of Coren with a weapon, though sheathed, begin to huddle in fear. She lets her guard down and relaxes for just several seconds in thought of calling out to Lawson and the Oracle of her find.

She turns her head ever so sweetly towards the exit before she hears a rapid shuffling and hissing sound that can only be described as the ruffling of clothes met with those same garments dragging along the floor. Turning her head back in surprise of the sound, Coren became face to face with the Lord of Death. Matah crooks his head while never losing his gaze upon Coren. And before Coren could question or say a single word, Matah finds his hand running up her neck; just over her red bandanna. As Matah lifts Coren off of the "sanctity" of *his* ground, his eyes grow large than small from within their sockets in anger.

"Something's wrong!" spoke the Oracle. Before the very eyes of Lawson and the Oracle, they witness Coren splashing, smattering and careening through the large window closest to them. Lawson can only cower away and cover his head from the torrential sounds of glass shattering and the traumatic sight of watching Coren fall. The Oracle tries to lean over to grab her but is helpless to aid. Coren, who is falling farther down, has only her last impressions of Matah in thought before hitting the ground. She wonders what he could be hiding under the large and thick veil that is wrapped around his lower face and upper torso.

Coren hits the salty and dried ground below hard enough to kill any normal human being. Matah steps through the entrance door way very casually. And without realizing neither that Lawson nor the Oracle are there, he jumps down after Coren confidently. In a shock to Lawson, he can plainly witness Matah disintegrate and vaporize, along the sound of hissing, while still in the air. The strange particles, which are made up of Matah, are black and hazy within a cloud of themselves. The remnants of Matah splash onto the surface below. Just as quickly as he fell, Matah begins to materialize himself. The black, grain-like specks are narrowing upward to form what looks like a head. His eyes appear so blank and wild above the veil that is wrapped tightly enough about him.

"By what Gods . . .? What is happening?!" Lawson spoke out in awe of such a sight. The Oracle answers, "It's Matah's power and ability. Along with strength, perhaps equal to mine, he can appear and re-appear by materializing at will. One moment he is whole and the next he can be several feet away or right behind you. Coren may have the will to take him on but all she has is her speed."

Though Coren remains motionless, she is conscious. She can hear Matah's transformation, who is taking his time at bringing himself together. While in no doubt of being in a lot of pain, Coren's broken bones are now snapping into place loudly. She is hoping that Matah isn't hearing her legs which are making the loudest of cracks like a tree limb snapping. Matah is proving to be arrogant which Coren knows can work to her advantage.

She peaks her head up just a little at Matah. Matah is just about finished materializing. He is leaner than Coren remembers. But he is oddly still a sharp dresser as ever with a suit and tie. He walks over slowly towards Coren. His round belt buckle gleams from the sun; blinding Coren slightly enough to mask his approach.

Matah speaks as he un-sheaths his sword with the diamond butt end and black handle, "You're alive? For one, such as I, to pronounce himself the Lord of Death: This is humorous. And if you are anything like me you're in a tremendous amount of pain while healing. Then the true question is: How fast of a healer are you?" Coren lowers her head face down. Matah brings the sharp edge of his sword upon Coren. He doesn't strike but contemplates on who she could be.

Matah has not a care in this world that this woman is one of his kind. And though Matah feels obligated to at least teach Coren a valuable lesson while seeing her as an intruder and trespasser, he knows that perhaps she can serve as a prime example of his strength and prowess as the Lord of Death through battle. So now he stands and waits for her to heal.

CHAPTER 8

MATAH ONCE TOLD Coren that it is not every day that Death resurrects a life. The self-proclaimed Lord of Death was the first thing Coren laid her eyes on in many years after Cassie's betrayal. It was Matah who found Coren in a chamber that was deep within the bowels of a marooned ship. And she was indeed submerged in a jelly-like chemical that made her unable to move. The history of that foreign mixture remained unknown to Coren until after she emerged from it. It was a solution that astronauts experimented with for deep space travel. When Matah discovered Coren while scavenging aboard the ship for what valuables it may have, he felt that the person within the chamber should go free.

It was that simple act of kindness that began the next chapter of Coren's immortal life. But it wasn't easy for Coren. When Matah used his immense strength to open the chamber, Coren was too weak to move or speak. She had not used her limbs for what seemed like forever. Coren didn't remember Matah carrying her from out of the ship and onto the beach where the ship previously slammed into. There, Matah made a fire and waited for the blonde woman to awaken. While not knowing who or what she was, Matah could only observe the mysterious Coren as she went in and out of consciousness. Her hair was very long and wild and she was very pale and thin. Matah waited a full day before she fully woke up. It was then did he realize that his company was more like him than human.

Soon her paleness surpassed greatly and she seemed more miraculously healthier than ever. With her long hair about her face, she had the most round eyes Matah had ever seen. In fact she was surprised to see Matah who was well groomed and staring right back at her. He was puzzled and wondering who she could be. She tried to stand when she realized that Matah was armed with a sheathed weapon; the notorious sword with the diamond butt end. Matah remained still. Coren's mind was racing in all directions. She eventually stumbled before the camp fire and fell on all fours. She breathed in the beach sand and air deeply as if for the very first time before staring up again at Matah. Yet still, Matah remained silent.

Matah used a mere hand gesturing of ease and calm as if to say: Easy, easy, and relax. He himself remained calm to treat Coren as if she was a wild deer. Matah simply didn't know what to expect next; especially from an immortal like himself. It didn't take Coren long to realize that she was at his mercy. But she herself had questions. Eventually the fire before her caught her eyes. Its rush of flames seemed to call out to Coren and twist the deep feelings within her gut. It was rage Coren felt for the one who betrayed her.

"Cassie!" Coren said harshly under her breath. Matah crooked his head and wondered what it was she said. Never the less he was pleased that she could speak and could possibly answer a few questions. Matah stood up and moved closer to Coren and the fire. Coren saw him more clearly. Though he was dressed in a suit and tie with dress pants and dress shoes, Matah bared no qualms with a shroud wrapped around his upper body which concealed his face.

He sat close to Coren who in return sat upright while almost being frozen by his stare. Coren knew that she was in fact still a dangerous woman and would kill this "man" if he tried anything funny. They kept eye contact, but it was Coren who was like a cobra who kept an extra eye on her company's sword. Its long and black grip handle was just in the right reach. She knew she was sure she had the speed but did she have the right angle to commandeer his weapon? While Coren was calculating being the dominant one around the campfire, Matah was merely gathering what words to ask.

Coren grew nervous and impatient. Suddenly she snapped while Matah caught her flinch before his eyes. She was too fast for him. As for Coren, what seemed relatively smooth was sloppy by her judgment. Matah felt his blade move and writhe from within his sheath. Coren knew that she was much better than that. What should have been left was the sound of the blade unsheathing itself. To her that was a sign that she was still healing. And within a blink-of-an-eye, Matah found his own sword positioned closely to the side of his neck.

Coren's hand shook nervously along with and down the long blade. Matah took notice yet remained silent. Coren broke the silence by saying, "I caution you: You'll die before this evening is through if you don't tell me where Cassie is!" He remained silent and motionless while only giving notice to his guest's increasing quiver. Matah gestured his hand as if to say wait or please. Then with that same said hand he carefully waved his sword further away from his neck. And with both hands he pulled down his shroud. Coren's mind, though it was still racing to gather itself and heal, quickly forgot she had a sword in hand against Matah who is at ease and graceful with a smooth face like hers. Clearly there was something more than human about him which caused Coren to let down her guard. But unexpectedly he didn't smile while watching with the glare of someone who has seen too much and has been around for too long.

He spoke and said quite plainly, "I'm glad that you are now able to speak. But you are obviously in no shape to threaten anyone. Please be still. You are not quite whole as you are frankly slow to heal." With that said, Coren fainted upon Matah who quickly stood to catch her. With her in his arms, Matah asked, "What is your name?" She breaths out, "Coren. My name is Coren."

Coren remained with Matah for three more days. They both ate what little they could find around the perimeter of the camp site. During their first venture, Coren realized where she was but something was off. If not for the wild animals that roamed off of the coast, she would not have of known that she is in South Africa. Yet from their scavenging on the second day, they came upon a deserted town. It was in complete ruin as what seemed like the sands were over-taking from all directions. The air was stale and was as if it were not used as if to say that the people there were once in a choking panic to escape. Matah seemed to pay no such attention to life that which hung from humanity's own noose. As there was some evidence of war with dried and spent bullet casings littering the streets, Matah did however pay attention to the details of the ill doings of humanity.

On the third day after Matah and Coren have gotten to know each other better, Coren asked, "What happened out there, Matah? What . . . year is this?" Matah, who Coren has come to know as a silent figure, paused before saying, "It seems you are fully healed and curious. That's good. So what year do you think it is?" Coren pushes back her long hair and answered casually, "The year I remember it being was 2034." Matah gave a long huff of a sigh. What he knew about the current date would surely affect his new friend negatively. With him being such a quiet guy, it didn't surprise Coren that Matah wouldn't answer right away.

Matah finally found the right words. His patients leveled the field once again. Matah said, "Be still, Coren, because I have a lot to say. The year is 2244 and much has happened since you were trapped within that chamber. So much in fact that it is like the sands of this continent which rolls and overlaps itself. Over time, most of Africa has become a desert where the central law of life is surviving the next day. Europe has gone 'dark' for quite some time along with its Western allies. But people persevere as they do along with those like us. Hmph. Poor humanity . . . A little after they re-established working energy and electricity around the globe, I suppose it wasn't enough. That's when a large scale war came about. That's when the Eastern half of the world used chemical weapons that will 'salt' our grounds for some time to come. The West, or should I say America, was slow to react to the cries of Europe. And as most of the Middle East remains off of the grid from nuclear war, all madness seemed to follow suit. America was then treating the world like a sinking ship. Currently from what I have gathered, they have isolated themselves from the world in order to survive."

Coren, who wiped tears from her eyes, said, "Have you ever believed that this world should have been ours, Matah?" Confused, Matah asked, "What do you mean?" Coren answered, "The one who put me in that chamber . . . The one named Cassie, who was once my friend believed that humanity's place was and should have always been second to us. She saw them as frail and unworthy creatures that deserved less. Perhaps she was right. How could humanity take something as beautiful as the Earth and trample on it?"

"I can see that you are upset, Coren." Matah sympathized. "But take what is left of the grass we have idly strolled on these past days. Is it not alive and beautiful as well? And yet, in some way, we are no different then it. We take up space, as it does, and strive to grow wild in reaching up towards the sun which gives us life. I personally have nothing against the people of this world. It's us, the immortals and those born with our strengths, that concerns me most of all. To further add to the matter: They can parish while we live on.

"Two hundred and ten years is quite an extraordinary length of time to lose." told Coren. "I'll be leaving on this day. I must see for myself what has become of this world of men." "I understand, Coren." said Matah. "But remember, nothing is as it was. The spirits and souls of others have become weak and easy to corrupt. And you must always be on your guard." Coren asked Matah, "May I ask what will become of you?" "I think I will continue to uphold my persona that is beginning to catch on around here." he said. "Matah, the Lord of Death has quite a ring to it."

From the time Coren left Matah she has been searching for Cassie. Along the way she has seen many things of this world including others like her. As the world, from once she remembered forever changed, it required Coren to change along with it. She eventually cut her hair short, as it is today, and acquired herself a short-sword since other weapons like guns are very rare with ammunition being more expensive. Most people find the simplicity of a sharp blade worthy enough to protect or deal damage.

After five years of venturing off alone did Coren find the whereabouts of Cassie. Not a beast, man nor other immortal like

Coren would stop her from confronting Cassie. That is what drives Coren. It is the reason why she sought after Lawson who she knows is the key to prevent whatever ill doings Cassie has in store with the Possessor who in turn has Lawson's guardian and mentor, Wesley. And with the help of her long-time friend, the Oracle, Coren is betting that she cannot lose.

But now she has a significant problem to settle: Matah. Coren thinks to herself that the fool doesn't even recognize her. Though Coren has healed, he shocking pain from such a drop on to the dry ground is still problematic for her. Matah draws his sword away from Coren and says, "Will you stand? I am curious as to what has brought you to my sacred land?" She doesn't speak which in turn is giving herself more time to heal. Matah says to Coren in anger and frustration, "Should I make an example of you in front of my new subjects? Since you *are* like me I could easily tare you apart over and over again. My new worshippers crave for a reason to continue believing."

"And what exactly are they believing in, Matah?" told Coren while slowly standing up. "You're turning them into *your* own slaves!" "Do I know you?" asked Matah. "There is something definitely familiar towards your presence . . ." "Yeah." told Coren as she carefully draws her short-sword out. "And I guess I'm here to help you remember." Feeling disgusted by Coren's bold answer, Matah says, "What! I allowed you time to heal and this is how you show respect?! I'll burry you before this day is done!"

Matah was once considered Coren's savior and friend hasn't a clue to who she is. And as deadly as he has proven himself to be on this day, he takes a hard swipe towards Coren's figure. But she saw it coming like any typical blow from an attacker. Instinctively she would have simply dodged away from the swipe of the blade, but Coren wanted to test the so-called Lord of Death's mettle.

It was easy to tell from Coren's quick reflexes, with her short-sword, that Matah's strike wasn't a strong one. He struck again but more loosely this time with an even weaker thrust. Their shimmering swords make the loud sound of metal crossing and pushing away from each other as Coren easily defends herself. "Who are you really? Are you from further East like Cassie or are you considered one who follows her?" While being caught off guard by Matah's mentioning of Cassie, Coren failed to see Matah grip his sword with two hands which is a sign that he'll have a much stronger advantage with his longer blade against Coren's shorter steel.

Sure enough, Matah, the Lord of Death, swiftly brings his sword up high and upon Coren's head. Coren focuses again while seeing the would-be blow in an almost slow-cinematic-view and is able to cross-block what could have been a devastating slash to the center of her skull. While holding the reverse edge of her short-sword, which is strategically dull, with just her other palm, Coren is utilizing the strength in her legs to remain planted upright on the ground.

As she stifles and shakes a bit, Matah is adding more of his upper body strength down on Coren while locked into her wide gaze. He is just beginning to remember. The determination in Coren's eyes after being reminded about her enemy, Cassie, is reminiscent of those three days she spent with him. In fact, when they spoke, Cassie's name would almost always come out of the lips of Coren. Though she had longer hair, her spirit was always as stubborn.

Matah begins to lessen is dual strength and grip on his sword which is giving Coren the advantage she needs. Like a lioness, she uses what strengths she has within to break free from Matah's sword-on-sword clash by darting his blade to the side of her while quickly slashing to his side abdomen. Sensing another opportunity, Coren tries to follow through with another slice across Matah's chest. As she comes inches from doing so, Matah de-materializes; allowing Coren's sword strike to wisp through aimless and ineffective. Like black puddles beneath Coren did Matah spread on the ground.

From high above on the cliff side, Lawson and the Oracle remain still and silent alongside the missing villagers who are all watching on. To see Matah perform in battle keeps Lawson and the Oracle on edge as the villagers are filled with a profound awe of their new God, the Lord of Death. When Matah came to McLander, he promised any who followed him that they would be protected from the coming times of humanity's downfall. He told them that he can shelter them from the on-coming Beast that preyed upon this world once before. The villagers couldn't have understood what Matah preached. But it was his immortality and supernatural ability that led them astray. Coren looks above at those spectating for a moment. She realizes that fighting Matah isn't going to be enough. In order to convince the villagers to return to their homes and lives, Matah must turn about his own words of who he really is.

The remaining grains of Matah move and slither further away from Coren. She can see Matah becoming whole once more as what was left swirled like a twister and thus became a part of him. He stood several feet before Coren and said, before an awkward silence could fill that space, "It's good to see you, Coren. I'm afraid that I didn't recognize you with shorter hair. But your eyes remain with that same determination. How long has it been since we last saw each other?" Coren answers, "It's been about five years, Matah. Five years of wondering this world for any hope or sign of Cassie. I know where she is now and apparently so do you." "If that is true," questioned Matah, "then why haven't you confronted her?" "I needed more assurance that I can stop whatever ill doings she has planned." said Coren. "You must know that she has come in contact with one of our ancient slave masters . . ."

"It is calling itself the Possessor and I am quite aware of that 'Beast.'" Matah explained. "In fact it is Cassie's meddling with that thing that convinced me to gather worshippers to head underground with before the 'fire', your enemy is playing with, scorches the Earth once more." Coren says in anger and disappointment, "Then I suppose that's it then. When Matah, the Lord of Death, faces the end and its darkness, he runs and takes as many humans along with him. Perhaps you were going to call your people 'the cowards of false pretense' and live in the subterranean city of 'disgrace.'" Matah interjects boldly, "Listen to reason, Coren, because you obviously do not understand everything. Cassie has become perverse in an ever growing attempt to gain limitless power. It's the same powers that the shell-less Beasts gave us. Some were strong as others, like you, were quick. Cassie believes that she can harness everything that the Possessor is capable of giving. Do not mock me in my pursuit of self-preservation."

"I will stop Cassie!" yelled Coren. "I'll personally put an end to her ambitions for power, Matah." Matah remains silent as Coren sheaths her sword. She says out loud, "I can win. We can win with just hope and perhaps someone as powerful as you on our side. And it doesn't matter that she is immortal like us. I'll bring her down through fear by the edge of my sword. Will you fight alongside us?" Matah pauses before asking, "Who exactly are the others you are referring to?" Not knowing how Matah will react to Lawson and the Oracle, as Coren did just defend herself from him, she is throwing caution to the wind by pointing out the two who are still high above. The rampant madness by the Possessor takes no discrimination towards immortals. "They are my friends, Lawson and the Oracle." Coren said.

Matah utters, "I haven't been like myself these days. I've dreamed of snow and promises, ill promises, which I refuse to believe. But what I do believe is that my mind and soul has become more tainted when I found Cassie in Africa. I traveled here, far north, to find that I am less at ease than I ever was. In these times of uncertainty one thing seems to have remained the same: You, Coren, carry a fool's burden. Revenge against Cassie is impossible. So what do you really want from me? To help you slay someone seeking to be the one true God of this world? For that, I cannot help you in your quest, Coren."

Coren, who is sad but determined, says, "Then release the villagers of McLander. If you know anything than there will be no hiding from what you call the Beast. For you to call yourself anything but a pet of our old, evil slave masters will definitely bring harm to yourself and your so-called worshippers. If you really want to salvage what will be left of humanity, then trust in me."

"Perhaps you're right." Matah told Coren while looking onward at the villagers from McLander. "What do you suggest I tell them? I did convince them well with displays of my ability to materialize at will. I told them nothing more but what I know to be true about this world and its future when Cassie becomes unstoppable." Coren answers honestly, "Then you should continue on that path with the truth and a little hope. Humanity's true salvation should first begin with a true direction. You and I are not Gods and if you wish to help those people or anyone else than you should be the first to admit to them your mistake."

The Legend of Coren

CHAPTER 9

THE GATEWAY PORTAL appears brilliant before Coren, who is less in spirits. She achieved what she wanted as the day progressed but her thoughts remain low. She didn't smile when she walked through the other side of the illuminating doorway with Lawson behind her. In fact she just kept on walking. Next, the Oracle proceeds through along with the lost and now found villagers of McLander. Everyone who walks in seems to pay no mind to Matah. The once self-proclaimed Lord of Death found himself as once again perhaps more like Coren; an oddity in this world.

He convinced those who chose to follow him that he was not a God along with the simple truth that he didn't know what he was. As well he was forced to admit that the Beast, he proclaimed to be mankind's undoing, was his greatest fear, but for good reason. Their brutal masters robbed the immortals' minds of their identities which further "chained" down any resistance. This left them with many questions as to who they were and how they came into the world. Matah nearly told them everything he knew that is true; which only leaves more questions to be answered.

The villagers found themselves tired and weak, physically and emotionally. They were filled with a life time of questions. To realize that they didn't truly understand their world was more than sobering. Before Coren convinced Matah to show them the light, their understanding of things was simple. Their ignorance towards Matah being a God was almost blissful for the villagers. To no longer fear the "dark corners" of the world under the wings of the Lord of Death, who stood before them, should surely turn any human into a fanatic.

Now the true sobering truth to why anyone would abandon their families in the name of a God that called itself Death: People can be stupid. At least that is how Coren puts it. Time and time again humanity has struggled to make fire for warmth, to cook their food, and to keep away what lurks in the dark; real or fictionalized. After moments of awe inspiring achievements and feats greater than themselves, humanity finds a way to put out their own lively hoods, their own sense of security, and inner flames. But Coren doesn't blame the villagers much for following Matah who struck Astor and betrayed McLander's trust. Being somewhat hopeful for humanity, like the Oracle, Coren also feels a sense of pity for Matah.

Matah was driven by fear of the unknown which has become a rare feeling for many immortals for thousands of years ever since those like Coren banished their soul-less slavers. Matah wasn't one of the original immortals to find a way to free his self, from what Coren remembers. Instead he was more likely another Beast's pet, to put it mildly, at a time when those like Coren spread the word on how to trap the spirits of their masters in deep and unrecoverable burials. It wasn't easy, as Coren saw it, but across the globe, there was hope and a chance for a new beginning; whether the human race will bend to their rule or not. That was the beginning of the end of true mysticism. It seemed as though the "wilderness" began to just fade to a whisper as the rise of humanity could not be ignored.

And poor Matah, under his strange and quiet interior, has kept his scars to himself. And now still with a long face, Coren looks back at her old friend and wonders what will become of him?

Suddenly Matah steps forth through the portal before it closes. Coren is a little surprised to see that he has chosen to come along. The Oracle takes notice and stops him from moving along with the rest of them. She asks in regards to the village of McLander, "Haven't you done enough? Astor's leg cannot heal unlike our wounds do and the people of this village will surely fear you." "Then perhaps I won't have much of a need for this." Matah responded while pulling down and apart his masking veil. The Oracle is unsatisfied with the fact that he is still carrying a weapon; the sword with the diamond end. Finding that she is starring it down, Matah says to quench the strong woman's fire, "And my sword, once a tool for my own gain, shall serve the people of McLander. Please consider my previous actions unworthy as today marks a new beginning. I only wish to humble myself and lend a hand where needed. And I'll only go forward if you let me . . ." "Come along, Matah." said the Oracle. "It isn't me you need to apologize to."

The group is just outside the village of McLander. With Coren leading the way she appears stuck in her thoughts. Lawson takes notice and realizes that they have accomplished a good thing today yet Coren seems lost. She trudges on quietly in a "place" that Lawson barely understands. What he knows is that Cassie maybe a challenge to overcome, according to Matah. It's unsettling for Lawson that Matah also mentioned a burden Coren holds against

Cassie for revenge. It is bad enough that Coren didn't bother to mention Cassie until later but that it is obvious that saving Wes is secondary. Lawson's mind is swimming in excuses for Coren since she is still going forth with helping him.

Maybe Coren needs to burry this hatchet between Cassie? But more so than aiding Wesley? She should have been more up front and honest. Yet how could Lawson know how big the world really is? Perhaps the conflict between Cassie and Coren is more at scale than anyone can believe.

Coren steps onto the village grounds of McLander triumphant. The youths of the village surround her in praise. She cracks a small smile from the corner of her lips and picks a small girl up high in acceptance of welcome. "She kinda looks like you, Coren." said Lawson. Coren says playfully with a wink of an eye, "I'm unable to have children so I think I'll make off with this one. What do you say, Uncle Lawson?" Lawson can tell that the old girl needed her spirits up again. The many young children then race and clash with their families. All of their smiles were enough to warm the hearts of any. Some welcomed their families with open arms as others broke down crying tears that said how could you abandon us?

Coren struggles with the thought of giving her little gift away. But she eventually let the girl go as she scuddles off to a man and woman who both kneel down with arms as wide as their smiles. The girl stops to pelt them both in anger and frustration before giving in to her deeper emotions. She smothers herself in their love while becoming lost amongst the rhythm of joy in McLander.

"You did a good thing today, Coren." said Lawson who finds himself beside the old gal. As they look on, they both couldn't help but feel good. But Coren knows that she still has an old score to settle. Coren reassures Lawson by adding, "Today marks the beginning of a new chapter for the village of McLander. They'll know all truths and for once I am just fine with that. I'm alright with this beginning for humanity here as that seed has been planted by Matah. They'll know we exist. Maybe this time it'll go right."

Suddenly Matah steps forth alongside the Oracle. All of the villagers take notice with wide eyes in confusion. Matah's every move is monitored in fear while others usher their little young ones away. It is as if the air is sucked right out of the souls of the people. They can only anticipate the worst from Matah who challenged them and their beliefs while finally striking down the proud elder, Astor.

Speaking of the devil, Astor couldn't help but notice his people in another tense moment with the immortal, Matah. He steps down from the large sanctuary he devoutly keeps up and functioning. With his cane, he is able to slowly stride straight towards Matah; the very one who wounded his leg. He came within a comfortable distance before the immortal with a fierce gaze. His eyes were not of a broken man but one who holds all of the cards. Coren and Lawson watch as a silence unlike any other blankets through McLander while the Oracle steps aside. Everyone knows what will be said could greatly impact Matah who has no place in this scarred world. Matah has done enough damage, especially to Astor, as he holds his fate, for this moment, in his hands.

Matah tries to speak but Astor interrupts him with a wave of his hand. Astor says while gazing through the eyes of Matah who is clearly humbled, "Forgiveness is a virtue here at McLander. And if there is one seeking it more today, it is you. Perhaps there is something we can learn from each other's pride from when we first met. McLander shall welcome you, Matah, as long as you respect who we are."

Astor Finn knows more than what he says in regards to immortals. His casual and humble, gray hand is more calculating than anyone can imagine. He is not like the other people of this village who were easily swayed by Matah's show of immortality and supernatural abilities. In fact Astor wasn't surprised by Matah at all. He knew that one day someone like Matah would come. What Astor Finn didn't realize is that his pride would get in the way of protecting his village from such an immortal which nearly cost him his life. When all seemed lost, the Oracle, who was staying with Coren, kept a close eye on the village and realized she could help. But Coren, of course, had another agenda. With persuasion by Lawson, Coren was successful in keeping McLander full of its people again. Now Astor has another powerful ally within the confines of the village.

For generations, the secrets of the world have been told to those like Astor who finds his self to be the last in McLander to hold such truths. Truths told in a book on a stone slab in McLander's oldest and only sanctuary.

The Oracle can now feel satisfied that the people of this village are unified and that Matah has a more welcomed place amongst them. Coren sees her old friend walking towards her and Lawson. The wind blows as if it is trying to sway the Oracle's blonde hair about her body and face. In return, the Oracle allows the cool air to mask her rosy smile of the day's accomplishment. But it wouldn't have been so without Coren. The Oracle, who is still slowly approaching, claps her hands to applaud Coren. Coren shakes her head as if displeased.

"What?" Coren questioned bluntly. "What are you so giddy about?" The Oracle responds, "We turned things around for our kind and humanity. Albeit a small step. But this is the right path for you and I and the world. Just look at us . . . together. I've had a vision, Coren. One that reflects the events of which have rocked this world and to the future of things to come. And these things will directly have a reflection on all three of us." "'Oracle predictions' again?" mocked Coren. "You are no soothsayer!" Lawson interjects, "I think I would like to hear more."

Lawson is taken back to his nomadic tribe in thinking about Erika's Grandmother, Shay. Like the Oracle, Shay's visions just might be true for the skeptic, Lawson, to believe. Especially after all he has seen. But Lawson couldn't help but think of his Mother, Sabita, over Shay and Erika and the life he left, which is still waiting for him. The Possessor's grasp is so rich and indulging that it catches Lawson unaware of the Oracle who trails off in verbatim with he and Coren.

Suddenly he can swear that snow is beginning to fall. Its light and flakey, miniscule shards of crystals dig and burn onto the fabrics of his shirt. Lawson's eyes widen as his pupils dilate to what wasn't really there. He can smell and somewhat taste the copper-frost air which increasingly becomes caked in a silver smog. His heart beats not faster but louder to every thump as if to drown out the sound of Coren calling his name.

"Lawson?" questioned Coren. Lawson can be seen with his hand held out in front of him. He twists his wrist slightly as if catching something that can be easily caught, according to Coren. Coren and the Oracle stare at one another briefly before bringing their attentions back to Lawson. Lawson says bluntly, "We should go."

Coren says, "I think you're right, Lawson. The sooner we head back to the Center of the World the better." "Great." spoke the Oracle. "I just want to talk with Astor first then Matah before we go." The Oracle walks off towards the sanctuary where both Astor and Matah were last seen.

Though the village is at peace once more, Coren's thoughts are centered on the very question of how long? Lawson interrupts the silence between the two of them by saying, "Revenge is something my nomadic tribe can be familiar with. I guess all of humanity can possess such distasteful feelings for one another." Coren turns her back away from Lawson and frowns. She says shortly, "I'm not human, Lawson." Lawson pauses to choose his words more selectively before uttering, "Wes is the only living family I have left and it seems as though your intentions are more revolved around staring down someone named Cassie." Coren turns around swiftly to face Lawson. Her wide eyes corner and dart to search his sockets. Her glare is like the barrel of a gun. But Coren knows that Lawson could not begin to fathom what the old girl is feeling.

Coren steadies herself and brushes her hair back thus allowing the strands to filter through and around as she strokes her scalp. After taking a deep breath, she tells the young but of age man, "Wesley *is* a priority. What Matah said back at the Dead Ruins about my burden being foolish was out of fear. Nothing has changed, Lawson, even as I have to admit that I am doubtful of our futures when I confront the Possessor. There is just so much you don't understand. I want to make things right between humanity and my kind. Cassie is what stands between us right now. If she does become more powerful or if the Possessor is free, there will be death amongst civilization and an even worse fate for me and the other immortals."

"You haven't told me everything, Coren. Like what really drives you to fear the Possessor almost as much as Matah does." said Lawson honestly. Coren answers, "Then you really don't know what fear is. Those like the Possessor just didn't control our bodies, they controlled our souls. They can read what's on the surface of your mind and when taken over or possessed, they can know everything about you. When this happens, it's unlike anything I can describe except hell. Our deepest fears, pain and loss are what they fed off of. Sometimes it is like that dream we have been experiencing where you can't see the snow covered forest through the trees. Before humanity's true reign, this world was more fantastic and mystical. From what I can remember there were those like myself, the immortals, who look human, as shell-less beings also roamed the corners of the earth's wilderness who called themselves what they wanted to be known as, like the Possessor. While vicious monstrosities and beasts became legends of facts and mysteries, humanity was becoming the truly blessed ones. Not just because the evil spiritual possessors chose my kind as their pets but because of your legacy and future. You also have to believe me when I say that humanity was the key to our salvation."

"We were the key?" questioned Lawson. "But how, Coren? I get the feeling that there is a lot more you could be telling me. You said you were a slave. Then tell me what that means exactly because it is obviously more than being in bondage to another for you and the other immortals."

Coren says very openly, "There were no early memories of a Mother, Father, or any family for that matter. Just us, them, and pain. There were five of us immortals without a name who kept a small dominion of this world under one spiritual master calling itself Kanthul. Kanthul and the other spirits were consistently at war with one another. They used us to rage that war. But the five of us were close and the Oracle is one of them. With our psyches compromised, for who knows how long, we had no past and were taught that there was no future while we were forced to obey. Kanthul was the sick type to tell us that it was more than generous to give us superb abilities. Abilities we had to use on other immortals unwillingly. We were taught hatred for anyone who stood in our master's way including humanity who Kanthul more or less ignored and saw as vermin. While most simple people were trying to understand or worship the dark edges of the fields and forests when something seemed out of place or struck them as a curiosity, it was us, the immortals in envy of your kind. We look like you and are able to blend in but were told differently by Kanthul that humans were the lowest of worms; easily fooled and weak. But it was a human who gave me the gift to fool Kanthul's ability to read my thoughts so I could get close enough to trap it within a crystal orb. That human gave no name but a purpose for me and a destiny for my kind to be free. Slavery has many forms, Lawson. For us immortals, our souls were in bondage and the not knowing of who or what we are burns through us until this day."

Lawson remains silent from Coren's words. He is a little embarrassed from questioning Coren somewhat rudely and brash. "You know that feeling you get that you said that's like pain or burning," said Lawson, "I can understand that it must be like you can't breathe or feel anything when everyone else around you cannot understand what you've been through. My Mother's remains are buried very close to my nomadic tribe's camp where you last found me. I think of her every day in respects to how you must feel, Coren. Like when you see a familiar smiling face and you just can't put yourself in that joyful state of mind. All I can say is that I'm sorry and that I do trust you have my interests in hand."

The Oracle approaches Coren whose sulking head is looking away from her advance. Coren says out loud to herself, "On the outside looking in . . ." She hears the Oracle's footsteps and looks up towards her to see that Matah is beside her as well. Coren knows what the Oracle is going to say before she utters a single word. Both of Matah's palms hold tightly his sheathed sword in one and his veil in the other. He swings the garment around his neck loosely as if ready for another fight. The Oracle says, "Matah has agreed to come with us to help in any way he can."

Matah says, "I am sorry about our past transgression and squabble. We're friends and I should have recognized you sooner, Coren. The Oracle has convinced me to accompany the three of you. She is as certain as you are that Cassie can be stopped." Coren smiles because everything should come together and work in her favor no matter the odds. But her aggressive personality cannot help but to push the envelope further though Matah *is* in her corner. She says like a predator that is closing in on her prey, "What you said earlier about my burden being foolish is more on the level if you have chosen to join us. Perhaps we should be more cautious of what words our sharp tongues flail about."

The Oracle recognizes Coren's hot and sometimes irrational temperament. They have come too far, time is not on their side, and it *was* the Oracle who convinced Matah to brave against the Possessor to fight alongside them. She is going to have none of it. The Oracle gently places her palm on Coren's shoulder and says to the both of them, "Well then, what I'm sure Coren is trying to say to you, Matah, is that words fail to express what deep gratitude she has for any and all help despite any past misgivings in spite of, and

I caution to say, in spite of not remembering who she was at first. So let's say we burry that in the past and move forward to keep this world from falling into the grips of an unparalleled evil not seen since any of us could truly remember. 'Sound good to everyone? I think this could work, really" Coren's temperament stabilizes like going from 60 to 0. She wipes the sweat that is between her nostrils and upper lip roughly as her eyes show that she has quickly forgotten and left behind the belligerent attitude with a more soft expression. Lawson blurts out a soft laugh from deep within his throat before uttering, "You're all mad."

As Coren begins setting in the coordinates for the Center of the World to travel to Cassie's known location, Matah reveals, "Before we head out, everyone should be aware that Cassie has a follower with her. I don't know who he is but he is another immortal and is well armed. He's as fanatical as Cassie and seems to serve under her like the edge of a blade. I suspect that we are going to have trouble with him the moment we get close to Cassie." The Oracle says, "One shouldn't be much of a deterrent against the three of us." "You mean the four of us." interrupted Lawson. "Wes is waiting for us and on my Mother's burial bed I swear I'll make things right again."

Coren remains silent while adjusting the final position for where the portal will open. She heard Lawson and the others but feels doubt in theirs and ultimately her success. Lawson, the human, is more vulnerable and susceptible to his very young heart and mind to being tricked by the Possessor. He'll have to want to save Wesley more than anything else. More so than any other desire once he is near the ancient and evil Possessor. If Lawson is compromised all will be lost. And Coren *has* taken notice to Lawson's preoccupied mind. Lawson must be strong when the time comes. But Coren has seen strength from the nomad that surprised her when they first met. Otherwise he would have been taken by Tomak and the desert wolves a lot earlier.

The bright doorway finally materializes like a slash from a mystical sword across the very air before Lawson. He looks away from the blinding abyss whose beauty draws him near until he steps through bravely. Matah is next as he quickly follows behind Lawson. The Oracle looks at Coren and says, "Don't think too much about this, Coren. Treat today's threat like anything else and we'll get through this." "I know you are trying hard to put up with me." spoke Coren. "But there is no room for error this time. Our chances are very slim despite what I've told Matah at the Dead Ruins. That you and I both know." The Oracle smiles a bit and says, "Than perhaps Matah's original plan wasn't so bad after all. We still have choices, Coren. We can choose to look away this time as humanity will no doubt be the Possessor's focus this time around. Just you and me." Coren walks towards the portal. Without facing the Oracle she stares through the other side and says, "No, I will not abandon this. Even if that means facing my past, enslavement, or oblivion." Coren's answer is short and sweet and everything that the Oracle wants to hear. Coren says with a determined glare in her eyes, "Let's go. Lawson and Matah are waiting."

On the other side of the portal, the air is as arid and dry as the ground the foursome find themselves walking on. Though they are back at the Center of the World, the sun remains at the same position as it was on McLander which is beginning to set soon. They are walking towards an unknown destiny to confront old demons. Below, the sandy ground has numerous foot prints on a wide trail that goes from one end to another as far as the eye can see.

Lawson's nomadic instincts begin to kick in while staring at the footprints that are low. He kneels down just enough so that his knees do not touch the rugged and sandy ground. He can further see that there are also many animal tracks amongst the adult and child-like feet. Everyone else begins to take notice of Lawson. Coren asks, "Is there anything special about the tracks, Lawson?" Lawson pauses for a moment. The harsh life on the Center of the World has taught struggling nomads many things like the necessity of finding water, navigating a weary family and clan to civilization by the celestial sky, and how to read tracks for the more than real stories they hold. But these ones in particular suggest reminiscent lore and danger.

Lawson says, "I can read these tracks like literature. From where we are at, we are not too far from the town called Shavi. Shavi is the closest settlement to where I left my tribe when I ventured off with you, Coren. Some of these tracks are very old as others seem to be a little more recent. This is definitely where Wes vanished." But then Lawson couldn't help but think of the shanty-goats he helped to feed at his tribe when he saw fresh goat tracks just a little from where he was kneeling. Strangely the prints end where another adult foot suggests that a person was sprinting or running. But from whom or what? On further analysis, the human track ends off of the trail without a trace, like the goat. Lawson walks further towards the very prints. It wasn't long when he saw, to his horror, a large desert wolf paw print that is bigger than his own hand.

Lawson backs away slowly as if the wolf is manifesting before him hungrily for the chance to taste his more-than-human flesh. He can tell that the paw print is fresh and hasn't been disturbed. The wolf that made that very print has to be close by. Coren questions loudly from a lack of patience, "Well, what is it. What did you find, Lawson?" Lawson gives out a long, whining, shrieking *shush* of caution which can only match Coren's confusion. Unfortunately,

Lawson's short and hot prayer to stay out of an earshot of the desert wolf that left its "Hancock" in the sand falls on deaf ears. That very devil of a wolf twists and crooks its head while sniffing the air to confirm if what it heard is real. The desert wolf's feverishly expanding lungs continue to grow and then deflate its mangled and hairy chest. This catches the attention of a larger female beast.

Her eyes glare and begin to sniff the dry air ever so deeply. Both desert wolves take little notice to the slow approach of a man who is close behind. The man calmly steps his dark boots in between the two wolves and halts. A gust of wind picks up bits of sand that brush his rugged jeans while filtering through the material's creases and folds. He shows concern for the desert wolves' interests in what he cannot hear or smell by loosening his very long hooded jacket in anticipation for what may lay ahead. This is more evident when he brandishes two sheathed swords on both of his hips. The large female desert wolf finally picks up the smell of Coren and the others. She walks cautiously over a sand dune to where she can now see the short haired blonde who is closer to Lawson. The male wolf continues slowly and low to the earth while letting out a growl from within its belly.

"Wait." said the rugged dressed man to the wolves. As the wind picks up harder this time, he places the jacket's hood up over his head and begins to slowly walk between the desert wolves who are obeying his simple command. Respectfully, he gently caresses the larger lead dog's back with just a touch of a few fingers as if to say good girl. He smiles darkly within his outer wear as he can see the others that are below the sand dune. Suddenly he grasps both of the dessert wolves' hair roughly and jerks them in Coren and the other's direction. They begin to race down and towards the four comrades like a chain being let loose off of two mad dogs.

"Look!" yelled Matah. "Up there!" As they each turned their heads up high towards the sand dunes that surround them, they can clearly see the two desert wolves racing down towards them and the rugged man who is standing against the wind which shows his very wide sleeves and long jacket swaying wildly about. Coren grits her teeth harshly while yelling, "Tomak!" It is as if she could smell him from up high on top of the dune. It's obviously an ambush and it has Tomak written all over it.

Without giving an order or pausing for any one's safety or grace, Coren runs stead-fast towards the base of the large dune. Both desert wolves zero in on her immediately. Coren's human-like feet begin to gulp and drown within the sand. She is working hard against the desert wolves' primal-engineered paws that are well adapted for almost any terrain. While trying to put distance between herself and her companions, Coren is resorting to using both of her legs and arms to push herself farther up.

The female desert wolf lunges from a good distance first. Coren quickly scoops a good amount of sand into a single palm and dashes it into the wolf's face and eyes before Coren rolls off to the side. She then takes out her sword and times the male wolf's approach with her special ability. Coren can see the carnivorous beast coming just inches towards her throat. To the normal and naked eye, the male desert wolf's speed makes it look like a dark ball of fur; growling viciously for a kill. But to Coren, it as if time has ceased just for her. The only thing stopping Coren is the advent of gravity on her short-sword. She slices the air cleanly and just short of the desert wolf's underbelly; striking its front leg dead in its tracks.

The wolf loses its balance and tumbles down the sand dune uncontrollably. Coren twists her head up at Tomak and gnarls her teeth in his direction. Tomak removes both of his swords from their sheaths and then unclamps their slim belt that allows the sheaths to fall free to the desert floor. The sun's glare wildly streaks across both of Tomak's razor edge swords. Coren isn't impressed as she continues upward. Tomak walks down to try and meet her half way. "Show me your face, Tomak!" bellowed Coren. "I was warned by Matah that Cassie has a follower whose mind is as bent as hers. I had a feeling it was you even before you tried to sick those dogs on us."

Tomak walks down closer to Coren with his boots sinking deeper through the sands. He doesn't seem to care at all that the terrain he has chosen to dual in is rough and gritty. To Coren, he looks over confident. Both are aged fighters and survivors who can read how the tide of their quarrels can go. But Tomak seems different, like any immortal that has been scratched by the evil Possessor. Coren stops climbing just a few feet away from Tomak who also halts. She tries to peek through the shadows of his hooded face just to see what his eyes could be saying.

In a bland tone of voice, Tomak says, "It doesn't have to be this way, Coren. We can be this planet's future. There is a movement out East that is spear-headed by Cassie to rebuild. Humanities wars have made the lands 'fertile' again for our kind to rise to our rightful place. We know that you can feel this. It is in *our* blood." Coren yells, "What are you saying?! I haven't heard of any movement except slavery! We shouldn't lose hindsight of who we are or where we come from, Tomak! What I think *and* feel is that this world's 'fresh start' can be for everyone. And what Cassie is doing now is wrong. Speaking of which, where is she." Tomak answers, "She is very close and she knew you'd be this stubborn when you return."

With wide eyes, Coren asks, "But how did she know that I found her in the first place? If she harmed a hair on Wesley, I'll . . ." "It is the Possessor." interrupted Tomak. "It knew all this time about you finding Lawson and getting aid from the Oracle. It drew all of you here for that human friend of yours."

Like a bolt of lightning, Coren turns around to view the chaotic scene below as the two desert wolves confront the Oracle and Matah. But something appears to be more wrong and dire with Coren as her mouth begins to stream a single drool of blood. She can feel something sliver cold and fine through the back of her upper torso.

She is stunned but doesn't look back or away. She knows now is the time to be strong. Coren knows now that Tomak has made his first move with just one of his swords. She tries to yell out Lawson's name but it only comes out hushed. She grits her teeth and knows that she must be vigilant.

The Legend of Coren

CHAPTER 10

THOUGH COREN IS immortal, she has always been slow to heal, unlike her friend, the Oracle. With the blade, held by Tomak, still in her back torso, Coren can plainly see the female desert wolf clamp its jaws down on the Oracle's arm. Matah is helpless to assist as he is fully engaged with keeping the now three legged wolf at bay with his sword. Then there is Lawson who is farther away from the Oracle and Matah, who without a doubt, is praying that the wolves do not take notice of him. Coren tries harder this time to call out Lawson's name. Nothing comes out but more blood. Lawson doesn't take notice of Coren. He backs away until he stumbles off of the trail and into a large and sandy hillside. "Lawson!" screamed the Oracle who tried to reach out with one hand in vain while the other is continuously being shook by the female's locked jaws.

Tomak says plainly, "Look at them and yourself, Coren. Do you really think you can stop Cassie or the Possessor from making her stronger? If our old spiritual masters have taught us anything, it is that power is the key. It was only a matter of time when we would take their place and no longer be known as pets. And this world will be ours with or without you . . ."

Coren is shaken by Tomak's words just enough to feel his sword exit out from behind her swiftly. She knows this will be her only chance to react before Tomak strikes again. There are many ways the fanatic could attack again with Coren being in so much surging pain as it is. She also knows that most likely Tomak will utilize his other sword in hand.

She throws herself forward and into a tumble down the gritty dune. As her momentum ceases, Coren watches Tomak retracting his other sword from what should have been the anticipated critical hit on her. It was a slice through the air which surprises him but not Coren. She immediately turns upward with the desert sands whirling and splashing about. To Tomak, Coren appears to carry herself faster towards him than gravity could hold down. He sees her almost in mid-air while leaving a cloud of grainy sand behind. He watches her as he can only block her single-sword-advance.

Coren, still with some blood around her mouth that has now dried, has become enraged. Furiously she cross slashes towards his chest again and again as Tomak barely tries to block the assault. She then aims lower while working her way up to his throat. Though Tomak has the high ground, he is forced to back further up and away. But does he dare throw in his mettle to show that he is still a worthy swordsman? Little does he realize that Coren wants Tomak to show all of his strength. She is in for the fight and she craves it.

Tomak crosses both of his swords to lock and then push Coren's away. They cease for a moment. Coren is breathing harder now along with Tomak. Tomak takes down his hood and says angrily while glaring at Coren, "Where is the pain I've inflicted on you?! Where is that scared nothing-of-a-girl I remember?! The one who causes trouble and begs for humanity's forgiveness! Or have you changed, Coren?"

"No, Tomak!" Coren yelled. "I'm still here!" Coren flinches while holding her short-sword at Tomak as if she is going to go straight into him. Tomak reacts by bringing both of his swords, parallel to one another, down upon her blade. In response, like a sidewinding viper, Coren turns her back to Tomak and twirls about to his side. All the while she repositions her blade behind herself thus driving Coren's sword deep into Tomak's side abdomen.

Tomak steps away as Coren retracts her short-sword from him slowly enough to feel every bit of the razor's edge. Tomak continues to stagger backwards until he is at the top of the sand dune. He drops both of his swords directly into the sand standing on their ends. He proceeds to fall on both of his knees and grips his wound with immense pressure. Though he was critically stabbed he is still able to speak. He tells Coren, "Puppets, we are all just puppets. It's like some kind of sick game with us, Coren. You may think you have won but how could you when not one of us can die! And all that effort you put out . . . For what?! So we can 'dance' to this all over again?! It's the Possessor, Coren! He is our puppeteer!!! And the 'song' called life will never cease . . ."

Tomak looks upward to yell again at God and whoever will listen but only finds Coren with both of her arms holding her sword up high and past her short blonde hair. That image will be the last thing Tomak will see for a while after he closes his eyes in defeat. Coren turns around and begins walking down the sand dune to leave Tomak lying still and behind. A strong gust of wind begins to bury him slightly. For Coren, decapitations are never easy.

What Tomak said during his "moment of clarity" spoke truth to Coren. The truth is that they *are* like puppets on a string dancing to the song of life. Everything is an unknown in this world except for Coren and her kinds' immortality and those like the Possessor who pull the strings. But are they meant to struggle and continuously fight one another? Or is there only peace through humanity's enslavement? If there is one thing that registers with Coren, here and now, it's the fact that she can make a dent in Cassie's plans to use the Possessor for whatever powers it may give her. She knows that it is time to rip the strings down from the Puppeteer and finally Confront Cassie for betraying her.

Coren walks down the sand dune confidently. Both of the desert wolves take notice of her immediately. The hairy beasts pair up together and away from Matah and the Oracle. The large female can smell Tomak's blood on Coren's blade. Coren, the old girl, still injured from Tomak's back stabbing and now feeling exhausted from their short fray, points her short-sword between them both. She quivers a bit but steadies her arm with her other free palm. The larger she-wolf glares into Coren's eyes who in turn stare back as if to say: I am not giving up!

The female turns around and slowly begins to trot away with the male desert wolf doing the same in a shadowed sequence. As Coren can no longer see them in sight, Coren drops to one knee. She says softly to herself, "They took my bluff." The Oracle and Matah rush over to Coren to see if she is alright. "What bluff?" questioned Matah. The Oracle answers, "Can't you tell that she has been hurt and is slow to heal? Those desert wolves were clueless to Coren's ability to take them on." Coren stands up and says, "Speak for yourself, Oracle. Those dogs have nothing on me! Besides, my wound is healing just fine as I speak." Coren looks around quickly to see only Matah and the Oracle standing around her. She walks between and away from the two while questioning plainly, "Where's Lawson?"

"Lawson!" bellowed Matah without receiving an answer. The Oracle says, "The last time I saw him he fell from behind us." "Lawson!" Matah yelled again. Coren walks faster to where she remembers seeing Lawson last. And there, where he fell, is a steep hillside. "Come quickly!" told Coren. "There is something against this hill." Coren swiftly climbs down the sandy and steep side that is off from the trail. What lies before her can be described as an old quarry with a winding path that branches into multiple pathways that go hundreds of feet down. As Coren hears Matah and the Oracle descending down the hillside, she turns to them and sees a large mine shaft entrance. It must have been dug out first when the quarry was created many years ago. Both Matah and the Oracle catch what Coren is staring at by simply turning their heads.

"Why would he go in there?" asked the Oracle. "Because," said Coren, "that's where Cassie is." The Oracle opens up again, "Sure, let's say Cassie is down there. But why would he venture alone? Something's just not right." "I can feel it too, Coren." said Matah. "It's as if something wants to be found. Something that shouldn't . . ." Without saying a word Coren leads the way into the dark abyss.

While Coren, the Oracle, and Matah cannot see what is ahead of them, they simply use the old mine shaft wall to feel their way through every step within. Cassie is there and what they feel is an energy somewhat familiar to immortals as it is old and unfamiliar to humans. As for Lawson, once again he is being manipulated by the Possessor whose influence on him grows ever stronger the closer he gets to the beast. What Lawson sees is not a dark mine shaft, which he is in, but a very bright tunnel with falling snow. It is as if the cold and snow are encouraging him to move further down the white shaft with darkness coming closer to him from behind.

"Lawson!" yells out Coren from far behind. Her voice echoes just enough for him to hear. "Coren?" questions Lawson. He looks behind and tries to see through the black nothingness that creeps closer towards him. In front of Lawson's hearing spoke the Possessor, "I was your messenger. Now I will be your deliverer, Lawson. As I have promised, I will make you God-like. Come forward, Lawson. Come forward to soon be in the caresses of your Mother."

Another voice begins to echo just ahead of Lawson. It's a woman's voice. Lawson begins to lose himself once more. He doesn't look back to the darkness and can feel the embrace of the snow-shielding light ahead. He knows it is his Mother. It must be his Mother. Sabita is waiting for him now or when Lawson is like a God. It doesn't matter now. Nothing matters to this poverty-stricken child who hated his own name, culture, and misfortunes. And how could he forget his own sweet Mother's voice so many years ago? She says, "That's right, my dear. Come forth and soon witness a new way and era."

Lawson takes one step of his foot followed by another. He can feel the welcome of a woman's hand on his shoulder. The snow begins to fade as if it was a cheap illusion to begin with. His eyes begin to dilate and adjust as if coming from the bright outside to the inside of a dimly lit cave, which he can now see that he is within. As he tries to look about, Lawson finds himself in a struggle with the woman's single handed clench. "Mother?" Lawson questioned before gazing on at the woman. "Not quite." she told him harshly.

The woman has a dark complexion and very long dark hair with bangs that cover down and over her eyebrows. Her stare above her thin physical body is very dark and cold. It is not Lawson's Mother, Sabita. In fact she looks nothing like the warm woman he barely said good bye to so many years ago. "Are you sober yet, boy?" she said low and gruff. "Or should I call you, Lawson. We've been waiting for you long enough." The woman jaggedly leans Lawson over a pit as if she is going to throw him in. He sees Wesley hunched over within the deep excavated hole. Though it is dark, he can see the back of his short, gray hair. "Wesley!!!" Lawson screamed. He sees that he isn't moving. Lawson becomes tearful as the woman smirks.

The woman says, "I don't need any introductions, do I? Your Wesley is still alive. He's just weak from being down there for a while. Let's just say that he and the Possessor have been playing a game of mental chess. 'The Possessor's rules, of course." "Cassie, please! Not like this. I was promised by the Possessor . . ." trailed Lawson in a guilty plea of omission. Knowing that she has the upper hand and feeling that she cannot lose, Cassie says, "That's right. Beg and get used to it. Our time has come. The era of the immortals is upon you humans. It was I who was promised by the Possessor to lead all into the future. But before I found the Possessor, I was considering expanding my territory from the East to this place you call the Center of the World when I was led here by the Possessor. But it was your precious Wesley who literally stumbled upon him first to where he lies now. Furthermore, in turn, the Possessor has possessed Wesley. Though Wesley grows weaker by the day from a lack of nutrition, I struck a deal with it. In exchange for its freedom, the Possessor has given me the power I wanted and the power I need to rule this world . . . Oh, and where are my manners?"

Cassie picks Lawson up off of his feet and over the large excavation ditch by his neck. Choking, he struggles but can only hear the sound of something fine and light dragging close to the side of Cassie from the dirt ground. Lawson's eyes widen as he can finally see that Cassie is bringing about a large sword that is similar to Tomak's. The dragging sound was its sheath scratching the ground. And though the sword is still within its holding, Lawson struggles more as he knows what is coming to him. Cassie is drunk with a blood lust that is unquenchable and says, "Your friends have failed you, Lawson. I've known Coren for a long, long time. And of course *she* has failed to stop me. But there is a bright side that even you, a worm-of-a-human, can appreciate . . . Well let me show you what I can do!"

"That's enough, Cassie!" beckoned Coren as she steps boldly from out of the tunnel and into the larger cavernous room. "I've heard everything. Now let him go!" Cassie pauses for a moment to the sudden surprise of her old "friend." Her mind is strongly tainted by the vicious Possessor and his promises. Her eyes begin to roll into the back of her head and disappear within an illuminating and unholy glow. The Oracle and Matah come forth as if they are drawn to a familiar and ancient energy being emitted by Cassie. It is something they haven't felt since those like Kanthul used immortals, like Coren, to rule its dominion against other spirit masters.

Cassie realizes that she is still holding Lawson and doesn't care for the demand that came from Coren. So instead she grips Lawson's neck tighter. Coren takes notice while Cassie says, "You wish for me to let him go? So be it!" With a surge of pure kinetic energy, Cassie merely opens her palm and releases Lawson who is struck by her power. Lawson sails and smacks the back wall hard and falls into the deep excavation pit ragged. In the heat of the tense moment, Coren yells out for Lawson but doesn't receive an answer. The Oracle breaks forth to charge Cassie with her brute force. With one clenched fist behind her, the Oracle tries to grab Cassie with her other hand. From the Possessor, Cassie was bestowed Coren's ability to concentrate her senses and heighten her adrenaline to move faster than any threat before her. With that fact unknown to the Oracle, Cassie is able to see and deflect the Oracle's open palm grab with both of her arms. Cassie was also given immense strength, like the Oracle's, as she uses it to kick her back towards Coren and Matah.

Coren tries to get the Oracle up off of the ground while Matah dashes forward with his sword towards Cassie. "No, wait!" Coren demanded as Matah ignored her in his own confidence. "She has other abilities!" Matah quickly found that fact out for himself. With one strike down and towards her arm, his perspective was baffling as Cassie moved about in anticipation of his blow. Suddenly her sword was drawn; clashing and toying with his. Matah struggles to block and finds his self slowly moving back with every steel beat to an endless dance.

Cassie steps back about a foot and with every ounce of adrenaline and speed she drags her sword through the ground towards Matah's legs. Seeing just the sparks and hearing what sounds like nails on a chalk board, Matah's only thought was that Cassie is trying to finish their "dance." So in turn, Matah dematerializes himself. As it is his utmost defense against almost anything, it is like his go-to-place when things go awry. That is until Cassie takes notice. Matah materializes whole again with his back on the gritty floor. Matah then witnesses Cassie's body stretch up high to the ceiling of the cavern. She lets out a horrible wail before her black mass rushes down and pours and inks a bubble around Matah. The black material, that is Cassie, begins to move and fester inward; suffocating and choking Matah in a now man-sized liquid cocoon.

Coren quickly leans the Oracle against the wall near the exit. She turns to Matah who struggles for freedom within Cassie's black mass. The Oracle says while in pain, "You have to end this. It's up to you, Coren." Coren runs towards what is now the abomination that Cassie has become and yells out her name in defiance. With her sword raised for a strike to free Matah, Cassie materializes several feet high; releasing Matah from her wicked grip. Like a dark cobra, Cassie then dodges Coren's first strike but fails to move faster than her light short-sword. Yet still drunk with power, Cassie materializes past Coren to reappear from behind her. And in her whole form now with sword in hand, Cassie says, "You should have stayed buried!" Coren turns around and responds, "Why did you betray me! Can't you see that our petty arguments are just history repeating itself again?!"

Cassie brings her sword up high and then down upon Coren who cross-blocks the blow. Cassie's strength has increased to its fullest which has surpassed the Oracle's. Coren can feel herself slipping her hold against Cassie's sword so she uses every bit of strength to drive the longer blade down and into the dirt ground. With so much hate-driven anger and over idealized lust for power, Cassie inadvertently buries her sword deep into the earth. This gives Coren just enough time to react by cutting straight through her arm cleanly. But Cassie never took her gaze off of Coren as her arm heals and attaches itself before it ever hit the ground. While Coren is stunned, Cassie takes this time to say, "You asked me why I betrayed you? It is because you simply didn't share my vision of a better world. What the humans have ruined, I shall start over. As for humanity, I don't see them going anywhere any time soon so why shouldn't they serve us. It's where they belong. We are strong, they are weak. It is the order of things. As for our petty arguments, I shall make this one our last."

Though Cassie's sword is well within the ground, she has no trouble pulling it as she begins to glow pure energy again. Coren boldly speaks, "And what about the Possessor? That Beast is the one who is truly pulling the strings. You're a fool if you think releasing it won't make a difference!" Cassie smiles wickedly and responds, "I have no intention of bringing anything out of that pit. It can stay there and rot for all I care, Coren, along with you and your friends. Of course, when I'm finished here with you, I'm going to seal off and bury all of you within this old mine facility with my new powers. I may not be able to kill you, but I have ways of keeping you out of my hair! Maybe I'll see you in another 200 years or so, Coren . . ."

Cassie strikes with the utmost speed which Coren can barely keep up with. While Cassie possesses many abilities, including Coren's focus power, Coren knows that she cannot miss a single step in defending herself as her adversary's skill with a sword is surprisingly superb. As they continue to clash, Coren is starting to wonder on how long she can keep this up. If it is true that Cassie won't allow the Possessor to become free, than perhaps it is enough. As Coren contemplates what she has accomplished, while still fighting against Cassie, from the time she met Lawson, to realizing that it was truly humanity's fault for why their world has gone sour, and to know that the Possessor is and will remain trapped, brings solace to Coren's mind and sense of being. With Coren's silver tongue, perhaps she might be able to convince Cassie to let Lawson and the others go. And since Cassie is indeed stronger now, then maybe no one is a threat to her anymore. With these thoughts running through her head, Coren also contemplates giving her life, and just *her* life, away to her enemy, Cassie. Even if it means losing more than another 200 years again.

Of course with such thoughts, Coren is unable to balance her offensive and defensive flow to battle against Cassie. It is like she is losing after admitting defeat in her subconscious. As Coren comes back into reality, she finds Cassie trying to disarm her. With a strong interlocking twirl of Cassie's steel sword through and against Coren's blade, Coren then sees her short-sword dashing against the side wall. But before anyone admits victory or defeat, Cassie, with just a wave of her arm, uses 10% of her kinetic energy to toss Coren against an opposite wall.

Coren tries to stand with every fiber and being in her against exhaustion and pain. She looks up to see Cassie standing over top of her. Cassie takes her healed boot and kicks Coren back over and down against the wall. "You know my kinetic power, which I've always had, was powerful, Coren." spoke Cassie as her eyes began turning white again. "Now imagine that 90 times over! I know you're slow to heal, so I'll sear your flesh off of your bones quickly!"

So Coren waits as Cassie begins generating more power. Coren can feel bits of her hair rising from Cassie's raw strength. If this is it for Coren, it is going to happen soon. Coren's own strength is gone and if she is only going to see darkness in the end, then she will embrace the abyss head on and unafraid.

Cassie senses something odd before she burns Coren's flesh. What she feels is ancient and familiar. Though she stands before Coren, with her arms stretched out with fingers crooked and ready, her attention raises suddenly to the corner of her eye. Cassie slowly darts her eyes to that said corner before turning her head. And there stands Lawson, shadowed just enough for Coren to see as well. He's hunched over and motionless but his eyes blink in a haze of red. There is an eerie silence that brews forth before Coren and Cassie realize what's going on.

Cassie turns her torso to face Lawson. Lawson quickly heaves his hands upon Cassie's head and face. Like a ragdoll, Cassie helplessly smashes into the wall next to Coren. Lawson begins shouting and barking dry words of a language not spoken in thousands of years. It is the same language that Jalil once spoke. The words came out of Lawson through spit and froth. As translated by Coren's understanding, Lawson says, "Treacherous pet! It is I who will bury you! And after all this time of coming close to freedom . . . I am finally free!!! All I needed was this young human's body to climb from out of that pit."

Coren remains still and silent in trying to draw as little attention to herself to Cassie's plight. It is the Possessor and it has possessed Lawson. The Possessor then places both of Lawson's hands on Cassie's shoulders. "What I give I can take away!" shouted the Possessor as Lawson's face augmented into a hideous grin. The Possessor begins draining Cassie of her special essence and powers. "No!" screamed Cassie as the Possessor uses Lawson's palms to burn fire about her shoulders. It wasn't long when Cassie is fully set ablaze by a bright blue and white fire that absorbs into Lawson's body. Cassie pleads to the Possessor as her body becomes weaker by the second, "You promised me. I'm the one chosen to lead! I was chosen for my people to lead them into a new age!! You promised me!!!

And here, within this man-made cavern, where the screams of Coren's betrayer, Cassie, still echoes, a plume of pure white light fills Coren's eyes. As she tries to peer through it, she sees Lawson standing by the exit. Suddenly a black smog manifests silently around him until it lifts him gently off of his feet; hovering the ground. Coren gets the sense that he has nothing else to do with this cavern as the world waits before him. With that attitude to embrace what lies ahead, Lawson quite literally flies out of the mine shaft and tunnel with extraordinary speed and vigor.

It wasn't just Lawson, but rather it was the Possessor who was craving freedom. It has been too many millennia to count since it tasted the air and the souls of immortals to enslave. One of the most evil creatures to manifest on this Earth is free to do as it pleases once again. Coren slowly and awkwardly stands up. She can see her short-sword across the other wall of the cavern. Something tells her that she is going to need it.

Just then, she can feel a strange and overly warm hand grip her leg. It's Cassie who is still smoldering, beaten and in pain. She looks up at Coren and says low in immense agony, "I was promised." To Coren, she looks all but dead. She is helpless and barely able to move. On further inspection, Coren notices that Cassie has become blind. Strangely, Cassie says a little louder, "You promised me . . ." Along with her sight being gone, it appears that her mental state may have been altered as well.

CHAPTER 11

"WHAT WAS THAT?!" questioned the Oracle. Cassie loses her weak grip on Coren's leg along with her sense of reality as her bitter friend moves towards the Oracle for aid. "Are you alright?" asked Coren who is concerned for the Oracle. "Can you stand?" The Oracle has healed physically but remains shaken as her mind comes to what has transpired. She doesn't answer Coren until she sees Matah struggling to get up and catch his breath. The Oracle says, "Did we . . . I mean the last thing I saw was a light that was so bright coming from . . ." Coren turns to Matah to help him to his feet while answering, "It was Lawson under the influence of the Possessor." Coren knows that there is no hiding from the reality that what they most feared is free to do as it pleases. It has become stronger from its captivity and no doubt hungers for power and devastation. It feeds off of pure fear, hatred, and sorrow. It is a Beast as ancient and mysterious as time itself with the primal feelings of jealousy for those with souls and shells as it has none to speak of. That is until it now inhabits within Lawson's body. And with his body, the Possessor can do extraordinary things.

A silent touch of cool air fills alongside the essence of the cavern. Matah and even the Oracle feel as if they have failed. Their eyes search the ground in defeat and woe. Matah and the Oracle remain still in their standing while thinking of questions like what if and what should we do now? But Coren has always had a stubborn determination in her spirit, whether it is to continue on or bide her time for another fight. The Oracle and Matah pick their head up off of the ground and watch Coren stride with bravado to her short-sword as if nothing strange or different has happened. She then places it into its sheath that is on her back and walks over toward Cassie.

"Coren?" questioned the Oracle as Coren quickly met the helpless and defeated Cassie. Cassie, who writhes slowly on the ground like a worm in the hot sun, is roughly picked up by Coren and brought to her knees. Coren, who is bent over Cassie and holding her by her shoulders, begins interrogating the sightless immortal. Coren says face to face with Cassie, "Where is Lawson?! Where did it take him?! Why does the Possessor want him so badly?!" Though the questions are valid for Cassie to answer, she does not. All she does is roll her head from side to side with tears streaming down her face. Matah stretches his hand out from a far, not in pity for Cassie but to Coren in his thoughts of hope being lost.

Matah says, "This is madness, Coren! It's too late." "No!" shouts Coren as she picks up Cassie and slams her against the wall and pins her there with a single arm. "She knows something, anything from having contact with that Beast!" Cassie cries and screams like a child in pain. Coren takes her other free hand and slaps Cassie once across the face. It isn't bravado Coren was demonstrating, it is hate. Matah says against Coren's passion, "What you're doing is senseless, Coren. We have to think about what is here and now. The Possessor's cage has been open and I believe we can still live our lives. It seems as though Cassie won't be a threat to you now. We're wasting our time here. Our kind has been through this before. We will survive this, like anything."

Coren opens up and yells, "She took a part of my life away from me! You could never understand how I feel! Cassie is a threat to everyone and above all else, she was my friend. And what about Lawson? We just can't give up on him! If Lawson falls or is lost to us, then so shall I!"

The Oracle stands behind Coren and tells her sincerely, "You must let her go. You must let *it* go. Matah has a point. We must figure out where we go from here on out. We'll manage as always, together. As for Cassie: She's given what was due to her with her sight. It would seem as though her blind ambitions was too much for her to hold on to."

Coren slowly releases Cassie who sluggishly slides down against the wall quietly. Matah walks over next to Coren and the Oracle and says frankly while looking down at Cassie, "And to think about all that trouble she has gone through . . ." The Oracle adds, "'How the mighty have fallen . . ." Soon Coren's balled fists unwind and relax as her fingers hang to her sides. She breathes a deep inhale followed by an exhale. Cassie huddles and shivers with her face still wet from her tears. She resembles someone who is caught out in the rain. But she is blind and mute as if trapped in her own mind. Perhaps it is just another staple of the vicious Possessor's mysterious powers. Whatever the case, Coren's pride has silently agreed with her friends that she must let go and move on. Now that Cassie is no threat and apparently worse off, Coren knows that she must honor Lawson as her first step in what she believes will be a dark chapter to come.

Though Lawson maybe lost to them, perhaps forever, at least Coren can finish his journey to free his mentor, Wesley. And still without saying another word, Coren walks over to the excavation pit and drops down within. There, she sees Wesley who appears very weak while lying down in the pit's cool and softer ground. But he is alive and whispers, "Coren, we knew you would come." "Easy, Wes." told Coren. "I've come to get you out of this hell-hole." Coren knows what she said, in regards to the pit, is just an understatement. She grabs and positions Wesley on her back before telling, "The only thing I need you to do is hold on. That's all you have to do and you'll taste freedom once more." "Freedom or ignorance?" said Wesley exhausted and more willing to give up. Though confused, Coren continues the painstaking task of climbing out of the pit. Coren acknowledges, "I'm sure what the Possessor said may have been true about those you worship and this world, but that does not constitute yourself for giving up or giving in to the madness it spreads. You and I share some things in common: The Possessor had us in its claws and that makes us survivors. When I get you out of here, it will be a new day and I hope you respect that for all of us who have survived!"

Coming to the edge of the pit, Coren finds the Oracle who is reaching out to her. While Coren uses the help of her strong friend to clear the deep hole, Wesley finds himself unable to hold on any longer. He collapses, but not before Coren can catch him hitting the ground. Wesley is indeed frail and in bad shape. And only God knows what the Possessor has done to him mentally. He says, "I mean no disrespects, Coren. I doubt that I had suffered worse than you did by the likes of the other monstrosities like Kanthul." "How do you know these things about Kanthul and its sufferings upon us?" asked Coren. Wesley answers, "The Possessor didn't just tell me . . . It showed me. It was in my mind and all I could feel was hopelessness. Before, I was traveling from the town of Shavi to my nomadic camp when my curiosity got the better of me. I found the entrance to this dug out shaft and began to chase down a strange glow. I fell there, in to that pit, and cracked the crystal sphere that trapped the Possessor. I didn't realize that, when I touched the orb, it cut me just enough to bleed on it a little. The blood is what allowed it to enter in to my being. Soon the Possessor became stronger as I became weaker. It lured us all here as it read my mind and realized Lawson was someone that it wanted dearly."

"Why did it want Lawson so badly?" Coren questioned. Wes replies, "To begin again the way things used to be before it was driven away into the orb. Lawson will be its first subject to lay a stage for many other humans to feed off of their fear and grief's, no doubt. But there is still something I don't understand which it showed while taunting me. The image still burns in my mind. What the Possessor desires most of all is a permanent shell to walk the earth in, but not in any manner that I can understand. Somehow it plans to find a permanent temple for its spirit."

"Then there is no stopping it from achieving whatever it wants." said Matah. Coren asks Wes, "It's alright, Wesley. I've seen and dealt with a lot in my time. But if what you're saying is true, then what or whose body are we talking about?" "It's not a living temple that baffles me." said Wes. "It's an unholy arrangement that deals with the dead." Coren takes a moment to think while the Oracle and Matah help Wesley to his feet. In no time, Coren realizes where the Possessor has taken Lawson. She begins to dial in previous places she has opened her portal before on her wrist cuffs.

"Lawson mentioned where his departed Mother was buried before. And it's not too far from here. The both of you, Matah and

Oracle, are right. We are wasting our time here. We'll manage against the Possessor like anything. And I know where we're going from here on out." said Coren. The portal opens to its said coordinates. The Oracle smiles and asks, "And where would that be, Coren?" Coren answers, "To where the journey began . . ."

As Coren prepares to walk through the portal, the Oracle stops Coren and glances over at Cassie one last time and says with Matah and Wes listening, "I'm all in with you, Coren. Just know that when the time comes, you won't be alone." Coren nods her head as if she understands her friend's words. She smiles and encourages the Oracle furthermore by saying, "I don't plan on coming back without Lawson. This is just as much his story as mine. They'll make stories up about all of us one day. And they'll know we tried to do what is right for each other." "For Lawson!" said Matah loudly. The Oracle follows suit, "For Lawson!" Coren orders while walking through the portal, "Let's get this over with."

With the Oracle carrying Wesley, she is next to step through the gateway. Matah can only give a resounding last glance at Cassie, who will remain in the old mine shaft, before he walks through the bright doorway. For Matah, he knows that perhaps a worse fate may await he and all immortals who oppose the Possessor.

Finding themselves still in the Center of the World, Coren, the Oracle, Matah, and Wesley are just outside the edge of Lawson's nomadic encampment. The nomads there finally take notice as the each step on to the grounds. Coren knows that Lawson must have come this way. She can almost sense that he is near. At least while she isn't feeling any doubt what so ever. The people there gather around in fear and curiosity to who the strangers could be and what they might want. Eventually they look upon Wesley who is too exhausted to speak up for himself. But as they come to recognize him, they gather around closer and whisper Wesley's name to one another; drawing more out from within their tents. Now it seems as if everyone is there including Erika and the nomadic elder, Shay.

Shay speaks for her people and says out loud, "Do not mind them, strange travelers. They only fear because of the weapons you carry. I can see that one of you has become ill or exhausted. All are welcomed here to simple rest. Especially if you have come to barter . . ." Shay walks closer and through the crowd who quickly disperse respectfully as she slowly passes. Erika accompanies closely to her Grandmother, Shay. Erika lays her eyes upon Coren's for the first time with Coren staring back. Not a word was said by Coren or the others as Coren fails to have the heart to tell them about the impending doom and death that might lie ahead.

Shay looks upon Wesley who is being held up by the Oracle. At first she doesn't recognize him as he coughs in pain. "What condition is he in?" asked Shay who looks at Coren for an answer. "Erika, bring water." "Yes, Grandmother." acknowledged Erika as she turns and dashes into a large tent. "Shay?" groaned Wesley. Squinting her eyes and peering closer, Shay's old heart jumps. "Wesley? Quickly, child! It's Wesley. Our lost tribesman has been found!" Shay tells Erika who comes from out of the tent with a bottle of water. Erika asks, "Did you say Wesley? Who are all of you? And what have you done to Wes?" The gathered nomads have gone from fearful to angry. Matah grips the handle of his sword tighter and says, "We mean you no harm." The Oracle adds, "We're here because of Lawson . . ." Coren weighs in for the Oracle, "It's Lawson. He's in danger as well as everyone in this camp. It isn't safe here."

The crowd begins to murmur against themselves while holding their children and loved ones tighter. "If you have brought Wesley back in good faith, then you all are truly dark messengers." Erika told solemnly. "Lawson has been gone for days now and is presumed dead. There is evidence of desert wolf tracks by the ruined city overhead where the only remains of Lawson is his handed-down outer wear that was given to him by his Father." "He's alive, Erika, and I'm sure he misses you dearly. He's dreamed of you during the nights he's been gone. He also misses his Father but most of all, his Mother, which is why we're here. I need to know where she was buried." said Coren. Shay says, "Your words are honest and I now know who and what you are. A recent vision of mine is now coming full-circle which involves Lawson. When the past intermingles with our present, a great change will take our people into the future. A new era is upon us."

Shay's words are haunting to Coren. The thought of a new age begins to echo in the old girl's head; straight from the book of Cassie. But Coren doesn't care. She apparently has a head start on the Possessor. The old sage, Shay, points towards the ruined city and says, "What you seek is out there." "Oracle, hand over Wes to these people." ordered Coren, "He'll be fine over here." "By the Gods, could it be that we are in the presence of the divine." said Erika in surprise. She immediately kneels before Coren while other nomads begin falling in praise. All except Shay kneel and bow their heads. As Erika begins to emotionally sob over the belief that Lawson is alive, though in danger, by the words of Coren, Shay places her old yet steady hand on Erika's shoulder. Shay says, "Do not bow to them because they are not Gods. In the vision I have seen, nomads will no longer submit to another false deity again."

Erika believes in her Grandmother's word, no matter what. But she is left confused as to who to believe in regards of Lawson. While coming up off of her knees, Erika questions, "Then what of Lawson's condition? And if these aren't Gods, then why tell them where our dead are resting, Grandmother? They maybe grave robbing scavengers." Shay looks upon Erika and the rest of her flock, whom some of which are still kneeling. Shay then says, "Everyone, do not be discouraged. I may not know all of their names, but what I do know is that these three are older than I am. Time and death has no weight on their souls. Most of what I have seen, in my visions, I cannot understand about our past and there place in it, but these immortals are friends of all humanity." "Thank you Shay." told Coren. "I just wish I could promise the return of Lawson."

Shay gently places her palms on Coren's lower face and looks deeply into her eyes, like a caring Mother, and tells her honestly, "For all the years I've been around, I've worshipped those like you when my visions told me otherwise thus seeing the truth. It wasn't easy, old one. And for all the millennia you've been here, you have followed your heart. Now it is time to continue that path."

Coren nods respectfully and moves out towards the direction of the ruined city. "So what's your plan?" asked the Oracle. Coren doesn't answer right away. She's trying to figure that out. "You'll have to trust me. I want to get between the Possessor and the burial site as soon as possible." told Coren. The Oracle questions, "We're not exactly going to dig up and desecrate a corpse so we can move it, are we?" "I don't think it will come to that. I just need to get there." Coren added. Matah says while he stops walking, "Does anyone feel that? There's a strong tremor about the ground like an earth quake." "That's no earth quake, Matah! Look, there before us!" Coren yelled.

To everyone's horror, one of the largest and decayed structures begins to topple down like a child's building blocks. Panic amongst the nomads can be felt as some scream in awe over such a sight. Yet strangely the earth continues to shake as another building crumbles before them amongst the sound of the last structure, smashing and screeching with metal and concrete being pulverized amongst the large plume of dust, sand, and debris. "There's no time!" Coren yells as she dashes towards the incoming whirl of sand and chaos. She has no plan and the Oracle and Matah know it. They've known Coren for her stubbornness and attitude, especially the Oracle. But it is her heart that she generally wears like a badge of pride. Matah, the Oracle, and Coren have been around for ages and yet know nothing about destiny or what things could have been or should have been. So if this, in the here and now, is an odd suicide run, at least they would try not to be slaves this time around. With Coren running in the lead, she will hold her own destiny in her hands and not let go until she sees it through.

The cloudy wall of sand and debris passes over Coren, Matah and the Oracle. There is an eerie silence within the gray smog. As Coren now walks through, the scenery has become completely blanketed from all sides. She can barely see Matah while the Oracle finds Coren by feeling around the thickly made air. And though the arid air is even drier than before, the dust and debris has made Coren and her comrades virtually invisible as the nomads cannot tell from a distance of the very danger they have put themselves in. But what everyone can hear is an unholy wail followed by what sounds like words formulating out a sentence. It's an ancient language of the Possessor; unheard of by any human of this world for thousands of years. But Coren, Matah and the Oracle understand it perfectly. The Possessor continues its out-cry, "For so many years I have lived in humiliation and defeat! No more shall I suffer the wound of not having a body! I have become stronger more than ever from my captivity! Now only I remain to return this world into darkness!"

Coren, who is listening to the Possessor's rant, nearly stumbles upon a mound of dirt and sand on the dry ground. She believes this to be where Lawson's Mother must be buried. As she looks to the Oracle, the Oracle is suddenly ejected off of her feet away from Coren; through the settling smog. With the Oracle gone in just mere seconds without uttering a single word, Coren turns to Matah. And as if something is grabbing him by his waist, he too is suddenly thrown back towards the encampment violently. The Possessor says freakishly profound in the language she and the nomads prefer, "Coren . . . have you forgotten that I can read your thoughts?! I am impressed that you have figured out my next course of action. The nomad's Mother's corpse will suit me perfectly. Your mind grows defiant by the second, Coren! You cannot stop me! It is impossible to destroy me. I am like the spirit of fear. I am the primal essence of what makes the hair stand on the back of your neck!" "Then you know that I'm not leaving without Lawson!" told Coren boldly out loud.

The dust settles all around. The Oracle and Matah find themselves several feet on the ground from one another. They both heal quickly enough to stand and witness Lawson, who is being controlled by the Possessor, walking towards Coren from the haze of settling sand and debris. Matah dematerializes and heads toward Lawson like a mass of skipping puddles on the ground. The Oracle runs to Coren's side as they both watch Matah pummel onto Lawson with such velocity, like a sledge-hammer, that it should have knocked him down. Seeming unaffected, Matah then wraps himself about Lawson. The Possessor stops Lawson as Matah begins squeezing tightly. To everyone's surprise, the Possessor uses Lawson to break apart Matah into many pieces that fall like glass onto the desert floor.

"Matah!" screamed the Oracle. She rushes straight for Lawson who begins to manifest a dark hue around its self. Coren, on the other hand, feels trapped within herself to do anything. She is sure that nothing can be done. Truly, she is believing that this is the end of her and all immortal freedoms. Coren wants to move her feet to assist her friend but finds that her fear keeps her immobile as if she's in quicksand. She can only watch as the Oracle wallops Lawson's body and face. It is to no affect, like from what Matah tried to start. But this time, Lawson's eyes begin to glow crimson as the black discoloration around him starts to boil and feed through and around his body which lifts him from the gritty ground.

The Possessor then strikes the Oracle with the dark, boiling smog. The Oracle tries to block it with her bare arms that turn red and bruised with every sickle-like passing of the ill air. She succumbs to falling down on her knees as the bruising worsens until she simply could not take any more. The boiling smog surrounds the Oracle until she couldn't be seen by anyone. Lawson can be seen hovering about the black mass which has over taken the Oracle. With a simple wave of his hand, the black boiling air releases her. The smoldering Oracle falls lifelessly to the ground.

Coren digs deep within herself and finds rage which lifts her off of her sinking and fearful state of mind. She dashes faster towards the possessed Lawson than Matah could. With her sword held in tow, Coren uses every bit of strength in her immortal body to swing her blade up towards Lawson's neck. It slices through an ink-shadow of the nomad which evaporates into thin air. Coren falls through the other side of the illusion and onto the ground. "You would really hurt him, wouldn't you?" spoke the Possessor who is standing within Lawson behind Coren. "Than that only makes you desperate!"

The Possessor quickly throws out, from within its dark mass, a boiling whip-like extension of itself that wraps around Coren's neck tightly. Coren uses her sword to try and break the strange and thick mass. The Possessor only grapples tighter and smiles wickedly through Lawson's face. The Possessor says wildly, "I don't need immortal blood to rule this world anymore since I am the only ancient dark spirit that walks its plain! With the body of Lawson's Mother, which I have chosen, I will set this world into a new dark age. No human worship will be enough! It is there blood I will seek. As for you and all immortals, what I want most of all is simple: I want to know how you feel when I hurt you and those you love!" Suddenly, the Possessor spawns boiling clouds of very long scythes from around himself. Lawson's arms move as the sharp and deadly tools mimic his gesturing. Coren blacks out and then comes to again just enough to witness Lawson's hand raising. She continues to struggle without air coming through her mouth from the whip. As Lawson lowers his arms in Coren's direction, the old girl blacks out for a second time.

Coren awakens to find herself ahead of a bright and swirling tunnel. All around her are unimaginable colors that appear to be guiding her attention to a bridge with someone on the other side. As she tries to look further at this person, it is like she needs glasses as he was without form. Coren takes a step to the simple yet beautiful bridge. Her thoughts can only be described as child-like and at peace in this world. Here, it is where time stands still and where Coren, for the first time, can let herself go into the carefree caresses of the beyond. Her first thought, strangely enough, is on knowing and expecting this.

While walking onto the bridge, Coren peers over her left. She sees still water more clear than anything she has ever seen. But then, there is her reflection which has changed, that brings about her second thoughts of what transpired last. She begins to remember vague and frightening thoughts about losing Lawson to the Possessor. Coren continues to stare at herself as the man on the other side of the bridge walks up to Coren. He says with Jalil's voice, "What you're wearing is as beautiful as it is special . . ." "Jalil?" questioned Coren. "You and all of this cannot be real. The Possessor has used false imagery before and I won't allow my emotions to get the better of me again." The man speaks, "You are half right, Coren. I am not Jalil but rather one who honors and respects what he was to you. The humans of this world are more familiar to call my kind Angels. My name is Sanriel and I am here to help you. This place and bridge, that you see before you, is in fact very real and with your will it will be the Possessor's undoing."

Coren tells honestly, "I still don't understand. Why do I look and feel so differently? Who or what am I, for that matter, and what have I become?" As Coren continues to look at the reflection of her now longer hair and beautifully modern dress, Sanriel steps beside her and gazes at his own reflection he has made to look like Jalil. Sanriel smiles and says, "I've been watching you for a long time, Coren. You must understand that I couldn't intervene in your affairs before. It was forbidden, and still is, to give the gift that I have bestowed upon you now. What you are wearing will protect you against the Possessor and for a limited time you will see it for the monstrosity it really is. I will give you these things because you are a part of us. Your Father is an Angel and your Mother is a human, like all immortal blood, you are what is known as Nephilim."

"But the Nephilim, from what I have known, do not exist, at least not anymore." Coren argues. Sanriel gives his answer by saying, "Ah, but they do. Within you and all immortals, they live." A strange breeze begins to intensify as the colors all around shift from bright to dark. Instinctively, Coren asks, "What's happening?" Sanriel responds, "Quickly, there isn't much time before the other Angels arrive. They may want to stop what you must accomplish." "What must I do?" Coren asks. Sanriel places his palm on Coren's shoulder and reveals, "I'm sending you back before it's too late. You must bring the Possessor across this bridge and I'll do the rest."

Coren can feel a very warm sensation throughout her body. It was like a baptism of warm oil that brought her sight into darkness. But she wasn't afraid nor felt alone. Consciously, Coren feels as though she is leaving a place that is thousands of miles away as a sudden surge of cold begins to sink in. And within this dark and freezing place, her mind begins to tell herself to awake once more.

The Legend of Goren

CHAPTER 12

THE POSSESSOR SMILES with glee without any reason to care for this world which has become like a leaf that has fallen from its Mother tree and into a descent of chaos and blight. As far as it is concerned, this world is up for the snatching. The Beast hovers through Lawson towards the burial den where many nomads have ritually honored their deceased by burying them into the ground with precious items and mementoes. This was done so that the dead, who are foretold that one day their souls would reunite with their bodies and walk again amongst family and friends, will remember who they are and to whom they belong to.

The nomads watch Lawson, their quiet wonderer of the beyond, the one who which fed their goats and had the presence of a gnat, begin to lower himself from the air. As he bowed his head, as if he was praying, no real words from the camp can describe the surreal presence of Lawson's power. They feel his energy that he seems to be emitting like standing close to a fire. He looks up towards the camp as people gasp with a cold and dry fear running through their spines. And though the possessed Lawson is a rather good distance from the nomadic encampment, he speaks well enough for everyone to hear, "What say you, Lawson? What would your Mother think if your sweet Erika were to be the first to see your decayed Mother last as I possess Sabita's remains to drain Erika's youthful essence so I can maintain a bodily form? As for the rest of your nomadic tribe, why let them go to waste. I'll feed on each and every one of them!"

The Possessor lowers Lawson's hands onto the ground. His eyes turn dark as a surge of energy washes from his arms and down into the earth. The Beast is so sure of its self that its time has come, so much so, that the Possessor lets its guard down by not trying to reach into the thoughts of others within a small circumference. "Soon, soon . . ." drooled Lawson from the Possessor's own words. Just then, Lawson's eyes went from a maniacal joy to pure shock. It felt the presence of something warm and very much alive. What this is vexes the Possessor's old and vile mind like a thousand heart beats from a thousand souls, all of which are centered on Lawson's well-being.

Lawson's head lifts up and looks sharply left and right all the while the Possessor searches its mind for the stray thoughts of who this person or thing could be. "This cannot be possible! In all my time I've never felt such . . . hatred for me from the presence of an Angelic figure . . ." revealed the Possessor. You cannot be an actual Angel. Then you must be a Nephilim in nature to hold such power."

The Possessor cannot read anything more profound than the frightful nomads' minds that are farther away. Cleverly, the sly devil begins to read the thoughts of the nomads in order to get a better perspective on who this could be. The nomads, in turn, are astonished to see a bright and glowing figure in a mid-air dash towards the Possessed Lawson. Faster than any eagle they have seen and more brilliant than the sun, this thing leaves a trail of sand and gravel that is kicked up from behind. Within a mere blink of an eye, the Possessor side steps Lawson's body which is just a hair of a fraction from being hit.

A dusty plume of choking sand and debris starts to settle about Lawson's controlled shell. His eyes glow increasingly bloody as the Possessor gnarls Lawson's teeth to what he is witnessing through the shadows of the sandy grit. It can see a woman's long and wild honey hair sifting through the wind's wrappings. She turns partially around and towards Lawson. She glares past him and through the eyes of the Possessor defiantly. The Possessor tries harder to read her mind but gets nothing. It asks, "Have you nothing to say, immortal? Or have you come to witness your world's end?"

Lightning strikes and fills the air with the smell of an electrical storm approaching. The cowardly Possessor uses the odd distraction to swiftly strike the woman with a materializing sickle. Reacting faster than any man, woman, or creature has ever did on this planet, does the woman who swings about a very unique sword to block and hold the Possessor's curved claw. With a dual grip on the very long, double edge sword, she continues to scowl past the nomad's eyes. The Possessor should have known who this was from the beginning. But how could it be? He left this immortal sprawled about the desert floor in defeat. Now she is wearing a long white dress with gold braces on her upper biceps with a black, leather over-garment held together with double straps leading down to a single elongated gold breast plate. The Possessor, though confused, confesses, "Coren, pet, how you have grown. 'How you have changed . . .'" Thunder quakes the earth as lightning strikes again.

The Beast seems to be taking in a deep breath. It no longer can read Coren's thoughts and she has proven to be stronger. Coren knows this as she says ahead of her well-being, "Your time is short.

I am no longer weak and I know you struggle to find my thoughts!" "Insolent pet! I will crush you!" yelled the Possessor as another scythe lunges towards her. Coren quickly pushes the other away and spins around with enough force to bat the incoming projectile into the ground. She then maneuvers for its dark and inky extension and cuts it cleanly. The other sickle, that was pushed away, comes up high upon Coren and then down. Coren jumps back as a loud thud is all that can be heard.

With the deadly sickle plunged deep into the ground, Coren quickly slices its extension up. Both scythes begin to bubble and ink into the earth as if they never were. Lawson's arms open wide and stretch like something other worldly. His palms begin to close while looking up into the heavens where a dark vortex mixes with heavenly lights appearing. The same lights Coren has seen before. "This is not possible!" the Possessor shouted. "You are not divine!" The Possessor takes Lawson's hand and points at Coren as if to accuse her of heresy and bellows, "You are not even a saint! This goes beyond objectionable! I will not have this in my new world!"

Coren interrupts, "I can finally see you for the creature you are! Your revolting presence is no more than a slimy stain to this world. I can taste your desperation . . . Your time is up!" Coren sees the Possessor for what it is as the swirling vortex seems to have a pull on the dark and misshapen figure. The evil spirit within Lawson has a long snake-like tail with a serpent's head along with small horns about its head. It is trying its best to hold onto Lawson with its scaly and massively long and muscular left arm. Its right arm is more freakish as it appears to be what can only be described as part of a tree stump with fleshy branches growing down from the Possessor's said arm. Its red eyes stare back at Coren, small and soul-less, as it shows that it is not going anywhere without a final fight.

From above, Angels watch as many of them fly to and from within the intensifying vortex. They are as fast as the lightning that surges and streaks across the dark clouds. As Coren watches them maneuver, she knows that she has a part of them within her. The old girl looks straight at Lawson, who is being pulled off of his feet, and takes off running for him. The Possessor doesn't have to read Coren's thoughts to know her intentions. It dispatches harpoon-like sickles whose sole purposes are to zero in and rip her apart. Like the Angels that witness from above, Coren takes flight and dodges the first, which smacks into the ground. Coren swiftly dodges the second and cuts its blackened rope before dodging the third which side winds and follows her from behind. Coren knows this as she veers up high atop of Lawson and the Possessor.

As the harpoon follows suit, higher up behind Coren, Coren descends like a golden hawk towards Lawson. In her brief fall, she sees Lawson's body which dangles farther off of the ground deadlike. His eyes are so lifeless that Coren, for a brief moment, believes that she is taking the ultimate risk in trying to save him, who may already be gone. With too many unknowns to think about within her lightning descent with a mystical harpoon giving chase, Coren closes her eyes and opens her arms to try and catch Lawson in mid-air.

Let it be known that Coren did expect the worst. She saw herself at her weakest when Cassie was at her strongest and then most vulnerable. She could practically feel the Possessor's deathly spike pierce her. But it is the Oracle, who is getting off of the gritty and dry ground, who witnesses Coren's triumph. The sharp harpoon drove itself into its own source. The Possessor bellows as it loses its grip on Lawson. Matah, who is in his whole form and lying on the ground, watches as the evil spirit that called itself the Possessor, claw the air in desperation before reaching the heavens where a bridge awaits its crossing.

The once arid air, of the Center of the World, turns cool and crisp rapidly. It is something that everyone can feel for miles. And suddenly a miracle happens: It begins to lightly snow. Matah slowly gets to his feet and slowly walks to the Oracle who is already standing over Coren. Coren is lying on her side with Lawson held close and tight to her. She and Lawson are still and motionless like the collecting snow that is on and around them. As she opens her eyes, she holds onto Lawson tighter. Lawson opens his sights which show that they are human eyes. He moves a bit and looks up at the Oracle and Matah as if to say that finally he is in a good place.

Coren releases Lawson gently and rolls over onto her back. The snow that now falls on her face is a testament to a miracle. Everyone within the vicinity of the snow fall knows this. She takes a deep breath and looks at the nomads who have gathered closer around. They may never know the true threat that Coren averted; except for Shay, that is. Then Coren stares at her two battered and war-torn friends. The Oracle smiles while Matah remains straight-lipped and quiet. Her friends, in their own way, are telling her that it is over. But then she looks upon Lawson. Lawson found more than what he bargained for about the manipulations and sufferings the immortals have gone through.

Though Coren knows that much healing and time will be needed for Lawson, his tears that run down his face from joy and sadness are actually a positive sign that he will keep his humanity and sanity. About a week later, Lawson was seen exhibiting extraordinary strength, like an immortal. Soon, Coren, Matah and the Oracle tested him to see if any part of the Possessor was left in him. It wasn't the Possessor, which was a relief to them all. Lawson can heal like an immortal and, with mentioned strength; it is like he is one of them. Coren did question loudly on why or how. The only logical explanation is that the Possessor allowed it. But for what purpose is anyone's guess.

After a month of such revelations, the nomadic tribe prepared to pack up their belongings and wander to another chosen destination and continue their lives of bartering and scavenging. Coren tried to convince their elder, Shay that everyone should travel to McLander with her. Shay full heartedly agreed as the others gave no grievances to leaving their nomadic lives behind. Long before the snow stopped falling, Coren knew what was best for Lawson and his tribe. At McLander, there are no desert wolves to speak of. And with Coren, Matah, and the Oracle there, they found a home that is protected. Astor and all of the villagers of McLander welcomed their new guests with open arms. Both Astor and Shay see this as an opportunity to continue their growth on this world as one larger community. Coren, herself, knows that both can learn from each other and perhaps widen their range in love. Both parties have many children and Coren is betting on that doubling within this less-than-hostile environment.

Coren now watches the on-goings of McLander from a distance. She's leaning against a tree that looks older than she feels. She can see Lawson, along with the Oracle, who is helping to build new housing structures for the formerly nomadic tribe that is now living there. Lawson is using his strength to lift and carry heavy tree logs to and from the site for the new homes. Coren wonders again about her friend, Lawson, a human with much untapped powers. Just then, Erika comes into view while playing with some of the children of McLander. It brings a smile to Coren's weary face to know that she has married Lawson. Lawson once referred to her as "biscuit" during the ceremony, to Coren's surprise. Coren could only imagine it as some sort of strange inside-joke. She now begins to think about the children they may produce in the near future and how beautiful they will be. To have a family *would* be the perfect ending, of course. She sighs and frowns and says, "What a beautiful life . . ."

A strange yet calming wind seems to try and mask the sound of feet walking through the grassy flora behind Coren. Coren looks to see a handsome man that she hasn't seen before approach her. He's wearing white clothes and seems to be not from around the area of McLander or the Center of the World. He gives no reason for the old immortal to worry so Coren allows his approach and continues relaxing on the tree in observance of the village.

"What a beautiful life indeed, Coren" said the man. "Have you forgotten me already? It must be this form I have chosen to show you which is my true self. I can tell that your thoughts are many . . ." Coren responds, "Sanriel. I didn't realize you could read minds. Are you here to take this stunning dress back?" Sanriel smiles and laughs and says, "No. It's for you to keep. And yes, I understand you're having many thoughts about Lawson, his life, and where that leaves you, an immortal. Or perhaps I should call you by what you are, Nephilim. Try not to be so jealous of Lawson and Erika's life together. He's more like you, an immortal, and will need your guidance. Besides, some love can last but for only so long, unlike Lawson's longevity." "He is immortal, like me?" Coren asked. Sanriel tells, "Not like you, Coren, but rather human still, in spirit. It is only by the Possessor's unholy craft that keeps Lawson inflicted, so long as the Possessor exists. Hopefully that will only be what is left of its madness. I'll keep a close eye on him and all of you, since being chained to this world *is* my punishment by the higher ranking Angels."

Coren says in a sigh of relief, "Then the madness has ended." Sanriel warns, "Not all madness is or has always been the same. As powerful as I am, I cannot understand why the Possessor would allow Lawson to possess immortality. Understand that no good can come of that. Especially from Lawson who has human thoughts and free will. You, Coren, are half human and half Angel. I must say that your noble actions have come from your Father's Angelic side. But when it comes to Lawson, this just isn't meant to be. But have hope. Things have a way of turning around for the best." "My Father . . . Can you tell me anything about him?" Coren asked. "I'm afraid that with being bound to the Earth, I cannot. But before Lawson approaches, there is one more thing I wish to tell you in good faith: Erika is with-child." said Sanriel.

With wide eyes in complete surprise, Coren turns to Sanriel but to only find he is gone like the gust of wind he rode in on. "'Talking to yourself, again?" Lawson jokes. "Come on, we can really use your help." Lawson gives his hand out to Coren who is sluggish to get off of the old tree. "That old tree is next to get cut down, though it does remind me of someone, in age that is . . ." Lawson continued to joke. Coren smirks and says, "You old dog . . . How 'bout you spread some of that love elsewhere. I hope it isn't a girl, for your sake." Lawson smiles while he shakes his head without knowing what she meant.

As Coren walks briskly ahead of Lawson towards the grounds of McLander, a small girl, who was playing with Erika, dashes over and gives her a big hug. Coren picks her up immediately and asks the child, "Do you like stories?" The little girl graciously nods her head. Coren then begins to say, "Let's see . . . How about I tell you the legend of how I met Lawson. It begins with the desert night sky shimmering ablaze from the stars above . . ."